Never Felt So Good

Rossana Campo

NEVER FELT SO GOOD

Translated from the Italian by Adria Frizzi

DALKEY ARCHIVE PRESS
McLean, IL / Dublin

First publication, 2003 Feltrinelli Editore Milano, published in agreement with MalaTesta Lit. Ag., Milano

Originally published by Feltrinelli as *Mai sentita così bene* in 1995.

Copyright © by Rossana Campo in 1995.

Translation copyright © by Adria Frizzi, 2020.

First Dalkey Archive edition, 2020.

CIP Data: Available upon request

www.dalkeyarchive.com

McLean, IL / Dublin

Printed on permanent/durable acid-free paper.

www.dalkeyarchive.com

Contents

There is no animal more invincible than a woman,
nor fire either, nor any wildcat so ruthless.

Aristophanes

Le donne come me
han messo il body a fiori
perché i tempi sian migliori.

[Women like me
put on their flowered camis
for the better times they hope are coming].

Gianna Nannini

Never Felt So Good

1.

THAT SCAMMIN' ASS friend of mine, Monica, has pulled another one. Time: nine forty-five a.m. and she's all wired and hysterical, she's already got a rap going that'd knock you out cold. Me, still in a coma from this brutal awakening, pasty mouth, frazzled thoughts, and she's yelling into the receiver: So, shithead, what happened to you? Up to nasty business?

I say, Nothing, a few dance-of-the-dragon exercises . . .

WHAAAAT??!

I repeat: Dance of the dragon.

Her: Dance of the dragon! Is that what we call it these days?

Her shrill voice pierces my head like an ice pick, I say: Look, forget I said anything...

She goes: No, no, no, you have to tell me what the hell it means,

Me: It's a Chinese method of circulating your energy.

Her: And I thought the old way still worked best,

Yeah, but this relaxes me,

I'd rather feel agitated,

Hey, I go, did you wake up this way or is this your normal state now?

Come on, cut it out, when did you get back, anyway? It's been a while, right, you just haven't gotten in touch with anyone,

No, I got back yesterday, I go,

So you were on vacation? In India?

Aaaahh . . . you know everything then.

I have my informants, she goes.

Who told you?

Monica changes the subject and goes: What the hell are you doing now?

Looking out the window, I say.

Out the window? she repeats.

Man, the sky today, it's enough to make you wanna shoot yourself. Paris is unbearable when it's like this. The sky's so gray, saaaaaaad . . .

Well, then you picked the wrong city, because the sky here is like this ten months a year. Maybe eleven.

Yeah, well, the Italian sky sure is different.

Riiiiiiight, she goes.

Look, in my opinion, when it comes to the sky . . . no one can beat Italy,

Yeah, except maybe Mexico.

Yeah.

Yeah, and the pizza, the songs, la mamma . . . HELLO! WHERE ARE YOU LIVING? Listen, drop the whine right there, I have lots to tell you. Forget about gray skies and blue skies. Seriously, I've got tons of stuff to tell you. Do you realize it's been more than a month since we've seen each other? I mean, more than a month!

I know Monica's tone when she's got a certain type of news to report, so I go: You didn't happen to meet a new man, by any chance?

We need to get together, I'm going to talk your ear off . . .

Come on, don't be a jerk, tell me something . . .

Uh-uh, no advances, we have to get together with the rest of the girls.

All right. Hey, I've got a bunch of stuff to tell you too, I say to one-up her.

We gave you up for lost, you know, she continues without a pause, we didn't hear anything from you before you left, I mean, what the hell, a phone call,

Nadia didn't tell you guys anything?

What would she tell us?

Nothing, it's good she kept quiet, I made her promise not to say anything, especially to you and Ale,

Hey, thanks a lot,

No, listen, have you heard anything about Lucia?

Lucia! God damn,

What?

Didn't you just ask about Lucia? Fuck, yeah, I've got some news about Lucia you're not gonna believe, I swear, you'll never believe it when I tell you!

Oh Lord, I go, what happened, wait while I get a cigarette,

Hey, what about the dance of the dragon?

Drop it, is she okay? Nothing happened to her, right?

Ale heard from her, she called.

Oh, so she's here!

HERE? Guess where she called from.

From Italy, I go.

Italy my ass.

Where then?

Perlin! goes Monica, badly imitating a German accent.

Berlin? What the fu—

Heh heh, goes Monica, sounding like she's enjoying herself immensely,

Why did she go there?

I know everything, what'll you give me to spill it all . . .

Come on, when are you coming over?

Whenever you want, not right away though, I have to put on my face first.

Four, I go.

I'll be there at three.

At two-thirty she shows up at my place. First she rings the doorbell non-stop, then she catapults herself inside along with several gallons of perfume, Monica wears a hell of a lot of it. I have to tell you, my friend is all about exaggeration, nearly five ten, thin as a rail, the kind of aquiline nose where you see first the nose and then her, a pair of hooves size nine or nine and a half depending on the shoes, then these green eyes, I mean, really green, an ex-basketball player's huge hands, and today she's even put on a bright orange and yellow-striped floor-length skirt with a punch-in-the-eye lime green T-shirt. To complete the outfit, a long hippie scarf with little pink flowers and huge seventies sunglasses that are completely unnecessary, among other things.

You definitely need those sunglasses today. It's gonna rain any minute, I say.

So, who's gonna hide my nose then, you? she says. We always greet each other this way, a bit on the rough side.

She also smokes these Philip Morris cigarettes that are long and thin, just like her. Monica and I have known each other four years. She's one of the first Italian friends I made here in this strange and hostile land. First she worked for a travel and tourism paper, she wasn't earning a dime, a miserable job, then she snagged this Polish guy who's a professor at the École des Hautes Études and decided to marry him and quit the paper. Now she doesn't do a fucking thing all day, she goes around window shopping, goes to the movies, hooks up with guys and cheats on her husband big time, that's her life. But she says she really loves her consort, it's just that he's Polish, and often depressed, whereas she's someone who wants to get the most out of life.

She examines her ass in the mirror, sighs and says: As far as I'm concerned, my ass is the best thing I've got, what do you think?

It reminds me of this girl from middle school who sort of looked like her, because she also had an incredible nose and always wore super-tight jeans and bragged about her ass. I wonder if there's a relationship between aquiline noses and showing off your ass, I ask myself. Meanwhile, Monica doesn't wait for my response and adds: Will you make me some coffee? Then she takes off her sunglasses, looks me up and down, and goes: You've lost weight, huh. Diet?

Right, a diet! I, who don't believe in diets but in psychophysical well-being, go.

So you really went at it, huh?

I say, Come on, tell me what happened to Lucia,

Looking like someone who would like to tell but won't, since she's too discreet by nature, she goes: Later, maybe . . . And she adds: Tonight there's a dinner at Ale's, but she says if we go we'll have to help out. There's someone new, apparently, some chick who studies math,

What fun,

No, Ale says she's cool,

Come on, man, tell me about Lucia, I go, pouring her coffee,

She grabs the coffee pot and fills her cup to the brim, saying: To hell with cellulite, you only live once. And then she adds: I'll tell you one thing, Lucia had an affair.

Finally! I go.

Her: That was the general comment.

With who? A French guy? I ask.

Listen, I don't like blabbing, because Lucia made Ale promise not to say anything. But you know how she is, she would have exploded if she hadn't told someone.

So, she decided to tell you, I go.

Exactly, she goes, very pleased with herself,

Yeah, right, the perfect person to confide in.

Well, I haven't told anyone so far,

You'll tell me, though,

Only if you swear you won't tell anyone else.

Count on it, I go,

Listen, I'll tell you just one thing, Lucia ran off to Berlin with a German, and from what Ale told me he sounds like he's straight out of a Mad Max movie.

Lucia with Mad Max?! I go, pouring myself some coffee.

Look, she must have changed, Ale told me that . . .

Damn, I go again. This really is news, who would ever have thought . . . I mean, I'm happy, if Lucia dumped her guy, I'm really happy, you know.

Hey, let's talk about me for a second, goes Monica.

Let's, I say.

I had an affair, too,

No! I go, feigning surprise.

An Irish guy, she goes.

Handsome? I go.

Handsome? An incredible hunk, meek as a lamb! Completely out of his mind.

And when did you have this affair, I ask.

It's a real recent thing, about ten days ago, last week.

Let's hear about it, I go. And she launches into a detailed account: wing span, arm and leg muscles, the flat, muscular stomach with six-pack abs like Michelangelo's David. Plus a tight butt equipped with deep dimples, which, I don't know how, but all of Monica's men have butts furnished with deep dimples.

Where did you find this stud? I inquire, not without a big trace of envy.

At one of Gisèle's parties. Just imagine, I went with Paul too, a big mess, but it turned out okay. Listen to this, though . . . And here we get into the hardcore details, with meticulous reportage on length, circumference and diameter. Monica's revelations are interrupted by the ringing of the telephone. I throw myself on the receiver panting, kind of dazed by the porn story. It's Ale, who says, So, you finally got back, I have good news and bad news, I'll start with the good: Lucia might be coming back tonight, she's coming straight over to my place.

Is it true she was in Berlin? I ask.

That bitch Monica has already blabbed everything to you, I see.

She's coming back tonight?

Yes, she's flying in,

I say: Wow, if Lucia is taking a plane then she's really lost her mind.

That's what I said to her, goes Ale.

What's the other piece of news? I ask, saying to myself: let's hope for the best.

The witch is back and on the offensive, says Ale, so I'm going to have to hurt her,

I go: Come on, take it easy, we'll be there soon. I'm here with the blue angel, she's got some news for us.

Let me talk to her, goes Ale,

No, I go, otherwise I'll have to hear the entire story about the Irish guy's salami again, I'm already all worked up.

So, you're coming over in a bit?

Yeah, yeah, I go, quickly getting rid of her. Then, turning toward Monica, I order: Keep talking.

2.

Upon completion of the anatomical description, Monica goes: Come on, get off your ass, let's get moving, I want to hear what's up with Ale and her rival.

I slip on my worn leather jacket purchased at the Clignancourt Flea Market for 150 francs, red jeans, also bought secondhand (50 francs), and I'm good to go. My friend looks me up and down, curls her lip contemptuously and proclaims: Okay, as far as elegance is concerned the French have never understood a thing, but that's not a good reason to go around la ville lumière dressed like a Tati salesgirl.

I push her out the door and we walk toward boulevard Raspail. We make our way onto the metro and she continues: Luckily here in Paris no one gives a shit about anyone, otherwise it'd be embarrassing to be seen with you.

I was thinking the same thing about her, but I don't say so. It's important to me not to hurt people's feelings.

We get off at the stop after Barbès: Château Rouge, and we head toward Alessandra's place in silence. I get kind of pissed at Monica when she starts with the criticism. Pure lachesis. I don't know if you're familiar with homeopathy, but this is a characteristic of lachesis, backbiting.

I say: Ahhh, when I get to Barbès I instantly feel good.
Yeah, just like you feel good in Dakar, or in Tunis, she goes.
Ale likes it here too, I say.
She declares: That's just disguised colonialism.

Ale and I shared the apartment in Barbès for a year. Then she met a guy from Calabria who was an instructor at a yoga center and they fell in love. Small detail: the yogi was married to a German woman and also had three kids. He dropped everything in five days, kind of like a sunstroke. So, the German woman didn't appreciate it, she waited for them outside their place and started slapping both of them around with the help of the three kids, who ganged up on the father, participating mainly by kicking and spitting. The German slaps hard, too, because this love of Ale's only weighs about a hundred and ten pounds (but with the right attributes in the right place, so she claims). Plus: she trashed the yogi's new car, keying it all the way around. She also got into the habit of delivering piles of shit to their front door, and it went on for months: piles of shit in front of the maison.

Monica is saying: Why, would you come back here to live?

Yeah, I'd come back, I don't like the faces in Montparnasse,

What the hell is wrong with the faces in Montparnasse, she asks,

They're white faces. Faces of people who've dropped out of the daily struggle for existence, I say lighting a cigarette, in fact, people who've never even been caught in the struggle and never will be. (Every so often I enjoy these anti-bourgeois rants).

She looks at me like, what the fuck is wrong with you today, throws her scarf around her neck and goes: Well, if you say so.

I keep going, though, because that's the way I feel today, I'm fucking pissed about society, and I go: Every once in a while, I find them kind of absurd, you know. They're always in lines, they form lines at restaurants, lines to go to the movies, lines at the post office, at the supermarket, and they're always alone. They don't even look at each other. They're afraid, if you ask me.

Afraid of what? she goes.

That they might have to give you something.

She says: Maybe.

Yeah, they're afraid that if they talk to you, they'll have to give up something to you.

She comments: Hm.

I add: That's not what life's about, you know?

I know, but now put a lid on it, or I'll shut you up with a punch in the mouth.

We ring Ale's bell and she comes to let us in all tan, black ringlets cascading around her face, her teeth and the whites of her eyes standing out like crazy, kind of African looking.

You fit in well with the neighborhood! goes Monica, who oozes envy from every single pore (another characteristic of Lachesis, envy). And then, in an increasingly shrill voice: Hey, you look so good all tan that those seven-eight little pounds you put on down in Puglia hardly show at aaaaall, seriously,

I say, What, you two hadn't seen each other yet,

No, just phone contact, goes Monica, you know, I've had a ton of things to do these last few days . . .

Ale has daggers in her eyes and says: Yeah, the usual things she has to do. And then, speaking to Monica's skirt she adds, What have you got on, the kitchen curtains? (The vacation in her native Puglia has brought back her strong Barisian accent.)

So, the German woman turned up again? Monica inquires,

Now she's calling every half hour, wait till I get my hands on her, I'll rip her a new one,

Come on, relax, says Monica, after all, I'd do worse if I were her.

Shut up, you of all people,

How about I make some coffee? asks Ale.

Not for me, I say, I'm already pretty agitated,

Oh, you'll have to tell me all about the kid, Ale says, turning toward me. Nadia mentioned it, but didn't go into detail.

That bitch! I go, she couldn't keep her mouth shut if her life depended on it.

Never trust girlfriends, says Monica. And then she adds: Shall we have a nice afternoon of girl talk? And lighting herself a cigarette: I'd like some coffee, though. A cigarette without coffee is utterly devoid of meaning.

Coffee gives you cellulite, goes Ale,

I KNOW! goes Monica, but for now, I don't have that problem.

We sit in the Pugliese-style kitchen, with blue ceramic plates, garlic and dried hot peppers hanging by the window. In the apartment next door, they're playing a Mina CD full blast. Are they Italian? I inquire,

No, it's a new guy from Congo who's crazy about Mina,

Jesus, goes Monica,

Do you remember that time, at the supermarket down below? I go.

When?

When we got stuck in the middle of a shootout between some Tunisian drug dealers.

Good god, Monica comments.

Well, so tell me something, says Ale.

Who goes first? asks Monica.

You start, I go, to create some anticipation among the audience.

Monica gets right down to it: I met the Irish guy at Gisèle's party. Paul was there too. I'll skip the detailed descriptions, otherwise this one's gonna bitch. All I'll say is that he's a cross between a young Helmut Berger and a blond Nicholas Cage,

Ale comments: Helmut Berger is a first-class fag.

I say: the idea of a blond Nick Cage is kind of revolting.

Never mind, says Monica, I'll tell you about my pick-up strategy. I see him sitting in a corner, on a couch, alone, smoking like a chimney, cigarette in one hand, glass in the other. I walk up to him and go, hey, did you know that smoking too much completely ruins lovemaking?

Dang, you jumped right in, goes Ale, her eyes widening,

And him? I ask.

And him, what a fool I was, don't make me think about it. He goes, I'm sorry, what did you say? And I insist, well, when you make love the taste of your saliva changes eleven times. When you get to the twelfth it means you're about to come.

You said it to him just like that? It means you're about to come?!

And you never saw him before?

And then I said: If you smoke a lot you miss out on all those taste changes, it's just like kissing an ashtray,

Ça alors! I comment, and him?

He was dumbfounded. But then he shakes himself out of his coma and says, with an accent just like Bono: I'd like to make love with you, but we can't now, I'm with Gisèle, she's my girlfriend.

WHAT??? You go to your friend's party and try to snag her man? shouts Ale.

Hold it right there. First of all, Gisèle and I aren't friends. Second, how the hell could I know they were together, they didn't even look at each other the whole night. Anyway, get this, he goes: give me your phone number, I'll call you tomorrow. I'm about to get a piece of paper out of my purse and he goes, no, don't let anyone see you writing anything, she's looking at us, just tell it to me and I'll memorize it. See what a scammer he is?

Oh jesus christ, goes Ale,

Wild, huh? Monica continues, all stirred up by the memory. As I'm leaving we say goodbye to each other and he repeats my phone number in my ear. I couldn't be more excited. That night Paul and I went at it hardcore. The next morning at nine I was asleep when the phone rang. It was him.

Holy mother of god! Ale comments,

Luckily Paul had already left, he had a conference in Austria, we made a date for that same evening.

Omigawd . . .

That afternoon, I'm totally agitated. I went to get waxed. Bought a new pair of panties and a bra for the occasion. Sat two hours with henna in my hair. Ran all over the place to look extra hot,

Yeah, okay, says Ale,

And then?

He comes to get me, punctual to the second. Real shy, all

jumpy. We go to an Indian restaurant in Belleville. A big ol'
candle on the table, lights dimmed, romantic beyond words.
We start talking, we're talking a lot of shit, we really don't know
what the hell to say to each other, we were just horny as rab-
bits. He looked even more handsome than he did at the party, I
could have eaten him up. A big Irish puppy. We guzzle a serious
amount of wine, I spew bullshit freely. At a certain point he
takes my hand in his and looks at me. You know those looks that
make you feel like the sexiest woman on the face of the earth?
Like that. After which he pulls me toward him by the hair, plants
his big lips on mine and we start making out like crazy. All of a
sudden something doesn't smell right,

What, you didn't like it? I ask.

No, the candle was burning my hair. I let out this bloodcur-
dling scream, everyone was looking at us.

What a klutz! goes Ale, laughing like crazy,

After the Indian food we go for a walk, arms around each
other. He takes me for a beer at a dive near the Bastille, where
we continue kissing big time, probably because we didn't know
what the hell to say to each other. So, to speed things up, it was
already past midnight, I go, hey, Kenneth, I didn't tell you guys
his name's Kenneth, I'm tired. Then I wait to see what he says.

And what does he say?

Nothing.

Your Irish guy's kind of dumb, if you ask me,

Yeah, duh, why the hell are you dragging this out, when she's
practically thrown it in your face.

Hey, thanks a lot, goes Monica.

3.

COME ON, LET her talk, I go.

How about we crack open a couple of cold ones?

Um, it's only five,

Five already?

Aw, come on, let's go for it.

Are we eating here tonight?

Yeah, keep going, goes Ale, bringing out the Heinekens.

You want me to go on?

What a pain, yeah, go on,

So the guy goes, Oh, you're tired? I'll take you home,

And what happened at home?

Not a fucking thing happened at home. Being with him in the bed I share with Paul bothers me, not to mention the fact that Paul has an amazing sixth sense and can sniff out anything.

What do you mean he can sniff out anything?

One time I brought this guy home, we were messing around on the couch for a while. He . . .

He who?

He Paul, as soon as he got home he started looking around and giving me these dirty looks,

Paul's spying on you, if you ask me.

Yeah, he might even have the house bugged,

Maybe even you.

He sews microphones in your underwear, hee hee hee, goes Ale,

He's listening to everything we're saying right now.

Morons. Anyway, I was saying: we say goodbye at the front door, and he goes, it's a lot nicer not to make love right away, it's more romantic, don't you think?

Are you serious?

That's what he said?

He's not a fag, is he?

I go, okay Kenneth, I'll talk to you tomorrow. I get home, go straight to bed and start tossing and turning like crazy.

Oh man!

I turn on the light, try to read something, turn on the radio, nothing. I try the pathetic route: manual tranquillizer.

Did it work?

Hell no.

Listen, if you're really wound up, it doesn't work.

You can totally wear yourself out, but it won't do any good.

No, in cases like this it doesn't work.

All right, go on.

To make a long story short, two-thirty, almost three, still can't sleep. I'm starting to get irritated. I tell myself, I'll try calling him now, but the fact is, I didn't want to impose.

Impose, you sucked face the whole evening,

That's exactly what I told myself, okay, we sucked face the whole evening.

And did you do it?

I pick up the phone and go, hey there, Ken! . . . Remember me? Were you asleep? Him: yeah, I took a sleeping pill. Me: well, because, you see . . . I'm having trouble falling asleep . . . I was kind of thinking, well, why doesn't Ken stop by my place . . .

Brazen hussy, Ale comments.

But he goes, no, no, I can't drive, it's dangerous with sleeping pills. Me: well, you know what I think I'm gonna do, I'm gonna call a taxi and come to your place . . .

You tart! Ale comments again.

I get up, put my clothes back on, redo my makeup, and there I am at five in the morning going to the Irish guy's house,

You're kidding, I go.

Where does he live? goes Ale.

On the other side of the city, near Père Lachaise. Anyway, the cab driver drops me off at the corner, because the street is one way and he's going the wrong way, he can't go around, he says there are some steps. I say it's not true because I know that street. We start to argue. Five-thirty in the morning bitching out a Parisian cab driver. I get out and say to myself, all right, it must be close. I check the address, it's number 129. I'm at number 1. I start hoofin' it. Pitch black, a pretty seedy street, no one around. At one point, two guys are coming from the opposite direction. Huge, they seemed huge, they had beer bottles in their hands. Without glasses I can't see a thing, I just see two hulks coming toward me and I say to myself, Here we go! Raped at five in the morning near Père Lachaise. What'll my husband think.

Oh god, is Ale's comment.

Holy fuck, is mine.

They come toward me, I'm about to pee my pants. They say something to me, but I keep going. I think: first thing, strike at the balls. Don't scream, don't try to slap or scratch, the things women always do. Go for the balls.

Oh christ, is Ale's other comment.

But the two guys pass by me without saying anything. I pick up the pace and after a century and a half I arrive at number 129.

Ale comments: The things people do to get some.

You said it, I concur.

Wait, it's not over yet, Moneek continues, I buzz the intercom, and talk about bad luck, here all the doors have a code. No, that one had to have an intercom. I buzz it and no one responds. I check the address again, street, number, all correct.

At that moment Ale's doorbell rings too and I jump in my seat. Ale darts toward the door shouting, Wait, wait, don't go on, okay,

Enter a chick with a little round face, long curly red hair. A plaid shirt and corduroys, she looks like she came out of a vacation advertisement for Ireland. She says timidly, Hiiii . . . What are you guys do—

Ale interrupts her saying: This is Valeria. You, sit down and shut up because we're talking some serious shit here. And turning toward Monica: Go on, don't mind her, she's one of us.

What, are you Irish too? I ask.

Her: Irish? No, why, what's Ireland got to do with it?

Monica, not minding her at all, continues: So, I ring and he, nothing.

What are you guys talking about? the new arrival asks,

Dirty deeds, Moneek goes,

She's having an affair with some Irish guy, Ale adds, at five in the morning.

So, what do I do, I go off in search of a phone booth. I walk the whole length of the street again, and finally find one. After two thousand rings the moron answers. Deep coma, he didn't hear the buzzer because he sleeps with earplugs. I go: at least take out the plugs till I get there, please. To make it short, I finally get into the boudoir. Inside the building it's surreal, like an old brothel or something, I don't know, it must have been something like that.

And what was his place like?

The apartment . . . Oh god, a dump, I couldn't see anything, it was dark, I just remember an incredible stench, the stench of a sleeping drunk mixed with intestinal flatulence.

Holy jesus! (This is Ale's other comment.)

He came to the door in a baggy pair of really sad, white underwear. Complete squalor! I enter and he sticks the plugs back in his ears and goes: sorry, but I can't keep my eyes open, I'm going back to bed. Hey, Ken, you took a shitload of sleeping pills, huh, I go. But he was already snoring like a pig.

WHAT? All that effort and he didn't even give you a little?!

Wait. I get into bed, at that point it's not like I was going to go home, you know. He's snoring contentedly, I get in another good hour of ceiling. When daylight begins to enter the room, I get up, pull down the shades, and finally fall sleep.

And that's it?

No, after a while he wakes up, all nice and perky, but I'm

totally out of it, my breath could kill someone, my back's a mess
and he's getting ideas about fooling around, right? Plus, he's still
got his earplugs in because he says he's really sensitive to noise.
The whole scene was so depressing. We started, but I couldn't
get into it.

No wonder, with a guy looking like that,

What a waste!

I look at the time, it's after ten. I rush to the john, get dressed,
and go home.

What a story! (This is my comment.)

And then? Did you see each other again?

What do you mean see him again, he's sadder than a Loach
film, man.

I wouldn't have cheated on Paul with a loser like that, says
Ale.

Enough already! I tried, I thought I was gonna have an affair
with some tall dark and handsome stud. Instead, it was just a
bad scene with a mental case.

Oh come on, every once in a while it's good to screw around,
it's just what the doctor ordered. (I'm the one who says this.)

I think so too, says the newcomer.

Think what?

Like Sade says, there are two possibilities. Either a man is an
asshole who views you as his property, in which case he deserves
to be cheated on, or he's a good guy who understands you and
doesn't ride your ass.

Where did this chick come from?

Are you sure Sade said that?

I've always said that if you sleep with another guy, you're not
taking anything away from your man, Monica clarifies.

It's not like you're giving away a little piece of it as a souvenir,
Ale adds.

That's what Sade says, that it goes against nature to become
a man's slave for the sake of love!

Damn, I've gotta start reading Sade.

Ale goes: Listen you guys, let's think about what to cook tonight instead.

Well, and what about your affair? Weren't you supposed to tell us something too? (Everyone is turning toward yours truly.)

What's this stuff about a little piece as a souvenir? I inquire to increase the suspense.

4.

A NICE PASTA, Sicilian-style.

And that would be?

Tomatoes, black olives, eggplant and peppers,

Whoa, nothing else?

It should also have capers.

That's it?

And anchovies.

My god,

Nadia and Betty will be here in a bit.

Wow, this is quite a reunion.

And Lucia?

Who knows when she'll get here.

Who's Lucia? asks Valeria.

A friend of ours, she ran away from home in July.

RAN AWAY FROM HOME! Valeria repeats like someone who's thinking: Man, these crazy women look like fun.

I'm also making you guys a quiche, says Ale, so we can find some solace from life's disappointments. We're going to dig into a nice pepper and beet quiche and that's that.

So now you're on a pepper diet? goes Monica, I can see why you've beefed up.

So you're on a domestic trip? I go.

I always cook when I'm nervous, goes Ale.

The last time you tried to make quiche it was like you invented some new type of plastic, Monica declares.

Hey, did you guys see what's happening in Italy?

No. What's happening.

Don't you read Italian newspapers?

No, thanks.

Oh, I don't do Italian newspapers anymore. Newspapers or TV.

I'm with you.

I'm through with that country. Personally, I'm sick of Italy, I mean, the Italians.

Hey, take it easy.

Oh no, I'm done with them.

Listen, let's change the subject, okay.

What about Gianni, where is he?

Who's Gianni?

Gianni is the yogi, Ale's guy

He said he was going out to dinner with his friends, goes Ale.

Riiiiight, friends! goes Monica. By the way, let me call Paul, I didn't tell him I was dining out. For once it's actually true that I'm having dinner with girlfriends.

Listen, this is no joking matter, goes Ale, her face all clouded over.

Oh, come on, don't get mad, says Monica.

I don't know why, but I have a bad feeling, Ale the sybil declares. Don't you guys ever just have a bad feeling about something?

She writes down everything we need to buy on a piece of paper, hands it to us and sends us off to make the purchases, me and the new girl. That lazy-ass Monica would rather fast than go trekking through the stores. We set off along rue de Clignancourt, me and the redhead, and she goes, Look, the weather has changed, now the sun is out,

Maybe it's all the bullshit we were talking, I go, to put her at ease,

Do you know Barbès well? the faux Irish girl asks.

Well, I lived here for a while, those were good times. Kind of rough, but good (I try to come off like a veteran).

The girl is an enthusiastic type. She opens her big blue eyes wide and goes: You know, I love Paris! Especially this neighborhood, you know what I'm crazy about here? I like those stands in the metro plus I like the Pigalle cafés, and the little parks, the ones with the old Arabs sitting on the benches, and the guys with the African clothes? I mean, have you seen that stuff? I'd wear an outfit like that too, what are they called? What do you think, could you see me in one?

Jesus. I turn on my x-ray vision and give her a thorough going over: substantial butt, strong shoulders, boobs on the small side. A good-looking lass overall. I say: Why not.

She continues, Listen, so what's the story about that other girl? Did she really run away from home?

I light a cigarette and say, You want to know the story about Lucia? Lucia's story is this. She's a friend of ours who's very, veeerry, square. She works for Arrêt.

Who's that?

Who's that, it's a publishing company. Lucia is the anal-retentive type, full of paranoias . . . Imagine this: little round glasses, hair pulled up, prim and proper business suits,

Is she blonde?

Why?

I was just wondering . . . I picture her as a blonde.

Anyway, we've been making fun of her forever. Because she's really ridiculous, the type who doesn't drink, doesn't smoke, suffers from gastritis, is afraid of flying and getting locked in the bathroom at a bar, can you imagine?

Wow! And she doesn't do anything to . . . she doesn't have a lover, or anything?

Sure she does. She lives with a guy who's a sociologist. He specializes in the study of prison systems, the discipline and punish kind . . .

Interesting. Don't you find him inter—

Wait, maybe I didn't explain him right. You should see this guy. He's the serious type, always caught up in his role. A fucking intellectual, one of those fucking Parisian intellectuals. Cold as ice.

Well, maybe she likes him that way.

She likes him that way! It's been five years, I'm talking five years Lucia has been with this guy. And do you know she hasn't even looked at another man?

I say she's shy, goes Valeria.

Shy! I go, she's totally out there! Someone who's so smart, so pretty, you know. Okay, she could dress a bit differently, it's true. Anyhow: she's very sweet, I think she could get as much as she wants,

Of what? asks Valeria.

Huh?

She could get as much as she wants of what,

Never mind, I go. Anyhow, that's not right, it's not true that she's never looked another man. She's been in a platonic relationship with this other guy forever, some French writer who publishes with them. A pompous ass.

He's no good?

The point isn't whether he's good or not, it's that he's a pompous ass, get it?

And so?

And so she's been seeing the pompous ass for a while now, they go out to lunch, every once in a while to dinner too, she's there drooling and he's never given her any! You see?

What hasn't he ever given her any of?

Jesus, Valeria, what do you think? Hello!

Ohhh!!! She goes like she's just made a discovery that will prove to be of vital importance in her life in years to come. Then she says: Yeah, funny he hasn't ever given her any, huh.

Whatever. Anyway, in July Lucia disappeared. This guy, the sociologist, whose name is Jean-Claude of all things, I mean, what kind of name is that, you can already tell from the name that he's an asshole, he called us all up. Now that she's flown the coop, he's lost his mind. Hours on the phone talking to us, asking us billions of freaking questions. Before, he almost never said a single word to us. When we went to her place he didn't even deign to look at us.

So what did you guys think?

Well, Ale was sure she'd gone off with the pompous ass.

The writer?

You're starting to follow, huh. Instead, nothing. The pompous ass didn't know anything either. Now she called Ale. Apparently she ran off to Berlin with some real wild German guy. She might show up tonight.

She goes: Man, what a story! And then she adds, You wanna know something? Before, in Italy, I was with someone for five years, too, actually six.

Seriously?

Yeah, we were like those little stuffed doggies you used to see in the back of cars, you know what I'm talking about?

Yeah.

When we broke up I felt like a jailbird who's just been set free. I felt like wreaking havoc, you know. Crazy stuff.

Mm-hm, I go.

So I came to Paris. I decided to study mathematics, it's easier to get a scholarship.

She's quiet for a while, like she's remembering something else, then she continues: I couldn't care less about mathematics.

Well . . . I go.

You know me and the boyfriend I had in Italy were supposed to get married?

You're kidding!

Keep in mind that I come from a small town, okay. I was almost resigned to it. I'd tell myself, well, we've been together so long . . . you know what happened to me instead?

What.

I was going crazy.

You were going crazy? Seriously?

I couldn't accept the old system anymore, I really couldn't.

But were you really going crazy or is that just an expression?

No, because you see, I think there's something that doesn't work the way they taught us. I mean, that it's natural to fuck the same person your whole life. That's not right, in my opinion.

Well no, clearly it's not natural. Why, you believed that?

This Valeria is pretty much off to a flying start, she's acting like she's just started to open up and is never going to stop. But we've arrived at the market and I'm trying to focus. She, however, continues without even coming up for air: Everyone used to say to me, my god what a great guy you've got, he adores you, he'd go through fire and water for you. And I'd ask myself, is this love? Two people who agree to destroy each other emotionally and sexually, to become mummified for the rest of their lives?

Whew, listen, Valeria, your linguistic prowess is impressive, I mean, seriously.

My friend continues undeterred: I never told anyone, there was nobody I could talk to about what was going on in my head, maybe I'm crazy, I'd say to myself,

And then what happened? Did you dump him? I go, smiling at the cute guy who's handing me the peppers and eggplants.

I had an affair with one of my female professors. Does that make you think less of me?

Yes, totally.

Really?

Cool it, I was just kidding.

I felt free with her, all those expectations, those paranoias weren't weighing me down. I walked around thinking: my god! I'm a lesbian!

Hey, what's wrong with that? Whitney Houston is one too.

Really?! Whitney Houston?

And lots of others,

I said to myself, from now on I won't be conditioned by love anymore, I mean, by what they want to make you believe is love.

Good for you, I go, and meanwhile I've managed to lead her to the egg counter. She's still talking: Shit, it's love that needs to adapt to me, not me to it.

You're one smart cookie, I say.

5.

I discovered something else. I already told you I couldn't care less about math,

Yeah, you told me, I go, passing her the bag of eggs while taking the change.

I discovered I really love women's accessories.

How do you mean, I say, a bit worried.

I designed some styles. Hats, handbags . . . Futuristic styles, to give you an idea.

For example?

She stops, puts the eggs on the ground and with her hands starts to pantomime something like birds flying around her head. She says: I've designed some hats with aerodynamic wings. And some handbags with blades incorporated, I'd like to show them to you.

Sure, I say.

What I'm interested in is creating items for women's self-defense,

Now that's an idea, careful with the eggs.

Yeah, I've also planned a line of fruit-flavored makeup. It's edible, if one likes.

Impressive. What do you think about that guy there, at the fish counter?

Who, the one with the T-shirt that says Kill your television?

No, the one with the fabulous smile, next to him.

But Valeria is staring at this black girl walking by, a sort of

miniature version of Miriam Makeba. This nutcase out on a day
pass from the loony bin follows her with her eyes until the chick
enters a café on rue Marcadet.

Anyway, I know I'm a bit repressed, she continues, for example, your friend, Monica, seems so free,

All appearance, I go, malevolently.

Wanna get some coffee? she asks, looking at the bar Miriam
Makeba entered.

We walk into the gas chamber-style café, packed with natives
from the hood. Kabil melodies are coming out of the jukebox.
We sit at a table and, looking around for the girl, she goes, What
about you? You got a boyfriend?

A boyfriend! I'm practically married, I say, rather pleased with
myself. I've been living with someone for three years.

Wow, I wouldn't have taken you for a married woman.

No, in fact, I'm not.

And your friend, the tall one? She sounds like she's had tons
of affairs, am I right? What about you? Do you have affairs, too?

Well . . .

Come on, spill it, she goes, as though we've known each other
since kindergarten.

Back in July I met this nineteen-year-old guy.

What about you? How old are you?

Shh, I go, turn down the volume. Thirty-one.

Did you know that nineteen-year-old males have a sort of
adoration for the female sex?

Ah, I go, impressed with the woman's ability to capsulize.

Then they get over it, she adds. Then continues: And your
boyfriend, what does he do? Do you get along?

My boyfriend, um, yeah, he's a couple of years older than me.

A couple?

Mm-hm.

Ten?

Um, a few more,

Twenty?

Almost. Let's say . . . well, yeah, you got it, more or less,
What's he like? I mean . . .
Oh, he's always off somewhere, he's a botanist.
A botanist?
Yeah, you won't believe it, but he specializes in tropical flora.
And ferns.
Ferns? I see . . . And wh-where did you find him?
At the Clignancourt flea market.
What?
We were fighting over a Chinese doll, you know those color-
ful little ceramic dolls . . .
No.
Come on, the ones that bring you good luck, there are dolls
for love, money, health, the usual things . . .
Uh-huh,
Well, I found this chubby little money doll, seated with her
legs crossed, smiling. I think to myself, I'm not letting this one
get away. I'm buying it. I start looking for the money in my purse
and along comes this guy, an Indian, not bad at all,
Indian as in native American?
No, Indian from India. He comes up and tries to take it.
Uh-uh, no way, goes Valeria.
I mean, money's no joking matter, you can't imagine how
long I'd been looking for this doll,
I believe it!
Yeah, so then I start arguing with this Indian guy. I go: hey,
listen, you don't get it, I'm desperate, this doll is my last chance
. . . I absolutely have to have it,
And him?
He laughs and goes: in that case, will you allow me to present
you with it?
He talks like that?
Yeah, just like that, he's an Indian who studied in the U.K.
Anyhow, I protest a bit, I say, no, I can't accept it . . . But he
goes, no, no, I insist . . .
And did the doll really bring you money?

Well, he claims it's a fertility doll. Monica says it's the conjugal love doll, I don't know if she was just making fun of me,

And you started going out right away?

Yes.

But when do you see each other?

All in all, over three years we've probably seen each other seven eight months, give or take.

Wow, and that doesn't bother you?

The fact is I've got to have my own space. At least, I think that's what it's about.

But do you think he's faithful to you?

How would I know, I think so.

You think? Don't you worry about it?

After all the losers I've come across in my love life he seemed like the first normal person I'd met. In the beginning I thought he was nuts, someone obsessed with tropical plants, you know, doesn't come across as the most normal person to begin with.

That's true.

But as soon as he realized he'd fallen in love with me he said so, you know? I've met guys who run away if they fall in love. Or who still have a mother fixation at forty. Or who as soon as you turn the corner they're already drooling over another woman.

Yeah, like, you think that's cool?

Then there are the ones who are afraid of getting involved, ugh!

And the Indian guy isn't afraid of getting involved?

No, not at all.

And you like that?

Hell, yeah, I like it. It's relaaaaxing.

Wait a second while I go order the coffee, no one gives a shit about us here. She gets up, smooths out her pants and goes up to the counter where the girl she had her sights on is sitting. She shoots her a look, orders and returns to the table, swaying her hips.

And what's his name?

Um, who?

Your boyfriend, obviously.

Oh, Gajanan, I say.

Gajanan! she goes, all happy.

The little Makeba is about to leave, she shoots Valeria a look, nods her head slightly, and winks at her.

Well? Go for it, I say to her.

What? she goes, blushing.

Didn't you see her? She winked at you, go for it.

Oh . . . no . . . look, I . . . I'm too embarrassed,

Aw, come on, let's go home.

I mean, there are plenty of people who are afraid of getting involved, plenty, she says again.

6.

WHEN I FINALLY pry the crazy woman out of the café it's six-thirty. We pass by a pharmacy and she stops to look at an ad for an anti-wrinkle cream. She goes: CBN, Cosmétique Bio-Natural.

What? I go.

I got some myself. It's an anti-aging treatment for the skin made with vegetable DNA.

Oh come on, you don't really believe that bullshit.

When I turned thirty I got paranoid. The night of my birthday I woke up and looked at myself in the mirror, I wanted to see if I already had wrinkles. I shone a bright light on my tits and ass, twisting around like a contortionist. To see if I had cellulite.

And did you? I inquire.

Let's change the subject.

One morning I went to the pharmacy with Monica, I say, we bought a bunch of shit, firming cream for the boobs, anti-wrinkle cream for the corners of the eyes, moisturizing cream for the body. A ton of shit,

Are they any good?

Go figure, I think they actually give you wrinkles.

Think about it, it could be a good idea, passing off a cream that causes wrinkles for an anti-wrinkle cream, huh, what do you think? We could do it, she insists. She takes another look at the shop window and adds, Listen to this, the other night I was watching TV, there was a documentary about Leni Riefenstahl,

Who?

The Nazi director, you know how old she is? Ninety-two.

So?

So she's fucking a forty-year old guy!

Hey, Valeria, you're not a Nazi or anything, are you?

Me? You're crazy, I'm an anarchist.

Okay.

I just wanted to give you an example of a woman who's aged well. Did you know she still goes scuba diving? I mean, she's ninety-two. She goes scuba diving, takes photographs and fucks a guy who's fifty years younger than her.

I say: You'll see, us anarchists age well, too, don't worry,

Are you sure?

You can bet on it.

When we arrive at the apartment I hear that Ale has put on Miss Perfumado by the great Cesaria Evora, and the other two, Nadia and Betty, are already there. We all exchange slaps and smacks everywhere, in our usual rough style. Even Valeria participates in the exchange, she seems to bond quickly with people, this happens a lot to sensitive types.

As for Nadia, I should tell you that we were very good friends for a while, the kind where you see each other every day thirty hours a day and then as soon as you get home you call each other. Then we had a falling out and didn't see each other for quite some time. After a while we started hanging out again but it was never the same, I think you get what I mean. We accused each other of selfishness, of wanting to recreate a symbiotic mother-daughter relationship. That's how she put it. I tried to describe the same concept using different words, a bit more vulgar. That's the problem with girlfriends.

I still like Nadia, though. She's kind of small and round, and when she laughs her gums show. She has round boobs and the rest of her is kind of round too: hands, feet, cheeks, fingernails etcetera. She works for French TV, she does a show for kids, one of those rather demented things, where she's surrounded by kids, puppets and little monsters. She even answers children's letters. It's hilarious. Because Nadia actually hates children. She started going with this guy Hervé, a dreamboat who acts in TV commercials, and at first, we were all wondering: how did such a stubby, round girl like Nadia snag herself a total stud like him? Then we met him and we learned that the stud is an uptight egomaniac with a brain roughly the size of a piece of popcorn. And we started saying: how did a nice, smart girl like Nadia end up with a blowhard like him?

Then there's also something to be said about Betty, who's a flight attendant for Alitalia and the only flight attendant I know who's four feet eleven in high heels, even though the truth is, I don't know many flight attendants. Ever since she and Nadia met, they've been best friends (as in totally symbiotic). Betty's the clueless type, one of those people who get something ten minutes after you said it, who always get the punchline too late, but she's very sincere and not at all malicious, like if she notices you've gained weight she tells you immediately, not to make you feel bad or take a dig at you, no, she says it just to make you aware of it.

So here we are all together, a bunch of expat Italian women, on this mid-September afternoon, with Nadia who's brought five pounds of ice cream and a bottle of grappa with a surprise in it, she says. And Ale is getting impatient because she claims the eggplant has to sit in salt for a while and the peppers need to be roasted on the grill and no one's volunteering.

Okay, if you want, I'll do it, says yours truly in the mood for heroic feats.

Hey, so is it true that Lucia's coming back tonight? goes Nadia.

Ooh, I'm so curious to see her, says Betty.

You've put on weight, Ale says to Betty, your face is all puffy!

She makes no reply, looks down and after a while says to me: You have some news too, don't you? Man, everyone's got something going on!

She wouldn't tell me anything, goes Monica.

She was smart, goes Ale.

So what are you waiting for, spill it,

I know! I witnessed the birth of the romance, goes Nadia.

So? Where'd you find him? asks Monica.

I grab a yellow pepper, wash it well and start to talk: the 14th of July, Bastille Day,

You were here? asks Ale.

Yes, that night I went to dinner at some friends of Teresa's, a bunch of wild British guys, theater people, plus the Japanese guy was there, the one Teresa always drags along with her, she brings him to parties, introduces him to people, and he lets her sleep at his place.

Is Teresa still homeless? asks Monica.

Yeah, I think she's seeing an Algerian guy now, but I'm not sure. Anyhow, we eat at these British people's house, and then we go out already half-drunk to raise some hell,

And Gajanan? Was Gajanan there, Betty inquires.

Gajanan was in the Amazon, because of the Amazonian ferns.

Hey, you can't be left alone for a minute, goes Monica.

Look, let's drop it. First, we went to the Port-Royal fire station,

To the fire station? asks Valeria.

Yes, on the 14th of July they have parties at the fire stations, Nadia explains, you've never been to one?

I continue: The atmosphere at Port-Royal is kind of lame, the Brits are drinking more beer and complaining because there's French music playing, they start shouting: French music sucks,

They're right, says Monica.

So, we drag ourselves to Saint-Sulpice. There was already more action there. Reggae reggae and the young firemen all revved up and red in the face, they're serving drinks and trying to pick up chicks.

Nadia says: the French are pathetic when they try to hit on women.

Ale says: Don't bite the hand that feeds you.

I continue: Teresa throws herself into the dancing. She grabs a guy and they start getting into it. Meanwhile the Japanese guy's feeling real bad, totally bummed, and I go, C'mon June, don't take it so hard, you know how Teresa is . . . How is Teresa, he goes. Nothing, you know, she just likes to have fun, don't worry. But do you think she loves me, he goes. Oh man, June, it's the 14th of July, a revolutionary celebration! Look, everyone's having fun, get with it, come on . . . So, he grabs me by the waist and goes: let's dance, you and me. I dance a bit with June, but god, he's shorter than me, I'm like a head taller than this guy,

You're such a racist, goes Betty.

Okay, forget it. I'm there dancing with this sad Japanese guy who's practically glued to me, and they weren't even slow songs. So I say to him, hey, June, wait a second. I look around for Teresa and signal her that I'm getting fed up, and she comes over to me. Listen, I go, it's not like tonight's my turn getting stuck with June, is it, I say, it's the14th of July, you take him back for a while please. Teresa grasps the situation and goes, hey guys, let's go somewhere else, let's head for the Bastille, there's more action there,

The Brits are happy, we start walking, every once in a while we stop at a bar to replenish our drinks, and I'm always on the hunt for a bathroom because I constantly have to pee,

Interesting detail, goes Ale.

Everywhere you look people are staggering down the street with bottles in their hands. We get to the Saint-Paul fire station where there's a ton of extremely wasted people, the smell of pot's so strong all you have to do is breathe and you're stoned. The strains of La Bamba mix with alcohol breath and the incredible stench of sweat.

Would you mind sparing us the details?

Oh, you're such a pain. Getting into the courtyard of this fire station isn't easy, everyone's pushing and shoving. Teresa and I are holding hands, first we get pushed to one side, we're smashed against a wall, then they throw us back to the other side, I can barely breathe, I'm thinking we're gonna die here. Finally another mass of people comes along and catapults us into the fucking courtyard. We end up right in this guy's arms. Man, I was drawn to him immediately, green eyes like a cat, incredibly green, a nose ring. A bandana on his head, pirate-style, and a bunch of tattoos adorning his bulging biceps,

Who was this guy?

Look, he was really young, eighteen nineteen years old tops. Teresa and I are pressed against him staring at him like a pair of dimwits, and he goes: who are you two awesome babes? I'm Gimmy! Hey, hi Gimmy, goes Teresa, drooling. And him, oh, Italians!

7.

Was he handsome?

Handsome? He was . . . he was the kind of guy you notice, I'll say that.

I don't believe it, Betty goes, the way you described him he doesn't sound handsome to me.

Wait, I saw him, Nadia goes, picture a whacked-out version of Johnny Depp.

Johnny Depp? No way . . .

Look, I'm telling you the truth! Remember the opening scene from Arizona Dream where he says he's checking on the fish in the New York bay, he likes fish because they know things, so he says, fish know things and that's why they don't need to talk. And then the music of that hunk Iggy Pop comes on,

You guys like Iggy Pop too?

I wouldn't kick him out of bed.

You guys are easily pleased.

Easily pleased with Iggy Pop? What the fuck are you saying?!

I'm going on with the story, okay? All of a sudden, this bunch of idiots doing a Conga line comes along, Teresa gets run over, they pull her in and drag her away, she screams but nothing can be done, destiny has decided.

Call it destiny!

This guy Gimmy and I are left staring at each other. Acting real cool, I get a load of these biceps bulging out of his tie-dye tank. You know the type with huge biceps, well-developed pecs, the kind you look at and immediately think forbidden thoughts . . .

Stop! Monica interrupts, stop right there! I know the type. Pumped up muscles, the kind that never lifted a book, just weights at the gym and motorcycle handlebars, at most.

How did you know? I go.

Come on, keep going,

You said he had green eyes? asks Betty.

Green with yellow flecks, I make a point of adding.

And how many hairs did he have in his . . . says Ale.

Come on, don't be so vulgar all the time, says Monica.

So Gimmy goes, come on, let's look for a place where we can dance undisturbed. He takes my hand, kisses it, and I almost die. He keeps looking at me, but every once in a while, he glances around, a la Robert De Niro, you know, and says: Unbelievable, man!

What a character, goes Betty.

He sounds like a caveman, says Ale.

And the way he fucking talks! says Monica.

Better than you, adds Nadia.

We start dancing, holding each other tight in the middle of the partying crowd, it reminds me of Karenina and count Vronsky's first dance, you know?

Yeah, just the perfect comparison.

So how come you're here? Shouldn't you have drunk rat poison?

You're such an ignoramus, that's Bovary, Karenina ends up hanging herself, right?

You're getting a little mixed up, Karenina winds up under a train. I mean, like she throws herself in front of one,

So who's the one who hanged herself?

Man, what a bad scene! goes Nadia.

Can I continue? So, we're dancing close, veeeery close, he's feeling me up discreetly, but nicely, I like it. He says something to me like, hey, last night I dreamed about you, hotlegs, and me: what do you mean you dreamed about me? We've only known each other ten minutes.

I dreamed a total babe was kissing me, and as soon as I saw you I knew it was you, a drop-dead beautiful babe!

The boy must have been really stoned, says Nadia.

Yeah, who knows what he was on to see her that way!

Thanks, thanks so much, I go. Nice friends, indeed . . . He's rubbing my back, then he starts rubbing my neck. The neck's the place that really turns me on, it can give me an immediate multiple orgasm,

What a crock!

It's just an expression,

Okay.

He's rubbing and rubbing, I'm starting to melt. He whispers in my ear: Listen, hot tits, shall we kiss now? I say, no, look, I don't think that's a good idea, and him: as Captain Sensible of the legendary Damned says, the important thing is to make the wrong music at the right time,

Holy cow! goes Ale.

Holy shit, goes Monica.

Weren't you thinking about your guy? asks Valeria.

Did you kiss? asks Betty, the romantic.

What was it like? Was it good? Nadia wants to know.

Ah, the kiss was super, I go, continuing to work with the peppers: soft lips, nice warm tongue going everywhere. Like eight tongues put together.

Never had a kiss like that, goes Valeria.

And did you consummate that same night? asks Monica.

Things were getting crazy, a fight even broke out, at one point he goes: why don't we go somewhere else? Me: like where? Him: like your place. And he smiles, he smiles big time and kisses me again.

What a guy! says Nadia.

A minor! What if they arrested you? asks Ale.

The telephone rings, interrupting my story, Ale gets up quickly and goes: What do you want to bet it's Lucia? Maybe she's already here.

Lucia! Betty exclaims.

From the other room we hear shouting and insults, like stop harassing me, what the fuck do I know about your money, etcetera . . .

Oh christ! goes Monica, what do you want to bet the German woman has struck again?

Who's the German woman? goes Valeria.

Gianni's ex-wife, Ale's guy, I go.

Oh my god! goes Valeria.

Meanwhile, I pour everyone a drink. Betty's shaking her head and saying, No, no, I don't want any yet, I haven't eaten anything.

Hey, since when do you not drink on an empty stomach? Nadia asks her.

Betty turns beet red and says, Oh, I'm trying to lose weight, you know, I've put on eight pounds.

Well, okay, but take it easy. Let's not get obsessed with the scale! We women are always obsessing over the scale, I go, with the tone of a Mary Woolstonecraf in her heyday.

Okay, continue with the story about the minor, goes Ale, returning to the table.

Who was it? The German again? asks Monica.

What does she want now?

Who knows, now she says she wants her money back, she says she lent Gianni a ton of money. Let's not talk about it anymore, it's getting me all upset,

I don't remember where I left off,

He kissed you.

Then he asked if you wanted to go somewhere else.

Yeah, and then I go to him: hey, Gimmy, wait, wait a minute. Him: what's the matter, baby? Me: I have to pee.

Again? goes Betty.

It was an excuse. I go lock myself in the bathroom, look at myself in the mirror, I mean, in what was left of the mirror, and I say to myself: what the hell are you doing? Are you kidding?

You talk to yourself like that?

Why? How else should I talk to myself? I was saying: calm

down, girl, now you just relax, chill out and go home. Alone. It doesn't seem too smart to go off on a whim like this, and what's more with some guy who was more or less in pre-kindergarten when you were in middle school. I splash cold water on my face and take off.

Booooo . . . my friends go in unison.

No, I think you did the right thing, says Betty, the only discordant voice.

So you left him there, just like that!

Poor baby, goes Monica.

And then what?

That night, the strangest dreams. I dream I'm on a beach, Gajanan is there, too, and along comes a pirate ship and these pirates kidnap me. Gimmy is on the bow and he's coming toward me, I wake up all agitated. The next morning Gajanan calls me, straight from the rain forest. How are you? Is everything okay? Did you have a good time at the party? Me, feeling like I've been caught with my pants down: WHAT DO YOU MEAN??! Him: Come on, I was just kidding.

What, you were already feeling guilty? says Monica.

8.

ALE IS HARD at work on the eggplants, peppers, anchovies and olives. Monica, idle as usual, comments: Let's hope something edible comes out of it.

Nadia states: Those who do, do it their way, those who do nothing have nothing to say.

Betty prods: I want to hear about the pirate.

Yours truly, who has moved on to washing the beets, continues: Two nights later the phone rings. A Sicilian accent on the other end of the line, hey, girl, it's me, it's Teresa, I didn't wake you did I? In a deep coma as usual, I go: No, it's only . . . THREE A.M.! Fuck, you're calling me at three a.m.! Her: look, I'm sorry, hon, you wouldn't want to do me a favor, something a true friend would do, just for tonight? That asshole June threw me out, he went into a jealous rage and threw me out. Well, you screw everyone but him, poor bastard, I say. So it's my fault if I don't like him? It's not like I have to give it to him just because he lets me stay at his place! Look, I don't want to argue about this at three in the morning, I go, just tell me what you want. I knew you were a true friend, she goes. Could you let me crash there for tonight? Tomorrow I can stay with this Algerian friend of mine, but tonight I can't because some of his fundamentalist brothers are there.

Oh jesus christ, Ale comments.

I try to cut the conversation short, I say, okay, come over, but make it quick. Meanwhile, I hear her saying to someone: sh, sh, I'll tell her in a minute. I sit up straight in bed, wide awake, and say, WHO'S THERE WITH YOU, TERESA? Her: listen, Gimmy's here, that crazy guy we met the other night at the Bastille, remember? He says hi. Oh, yeah, say hi to him for me, I go. Where the hell did you run into him? And Teresa: he also wants to know if he can see you tomorrow. I go, put him on. As soon as I hear his voice I feel butterflies in my stomach, I say, how are you Gimmy, oh, not too well, he goes. What happened? Him: You left me there like a jerk the other night, and me: w-well . . . Him: listen, shithead, I've thought about you a lot, I've been thinking about you for two days, if I don't see you tomorrow my head is going to explode.

You can totally tell that he didn't have anything better to do, comments Betty ever so nicely.

I say: what do you want to do, meet in a café? Him: in a café? What the hell are you talking about, no, man, let's meet somewhere more happening.

What does somewhere more happening mean? asks Ale.

I say to him: Listen, I was planning to go to the pool tomorrow, do you want to go with me? Him: the pool! Far out!

Hear that? She's playing the athlete for the kid, says Ale.

So? Is it against the law? I go, irritated.

No, it's just that you're so lazy, says Monica, who's the laziest girl on earth.

Ale goes: Hey, don't let the peppers burn.

Then I say to Gimmy: I know a nice pool, it's not far from here. Him: Cool! Let's go, man.

Oh no, you let yourself be seen in public with that guy! says Monica again.

Don't be silly, who do you think is going to see her there? says Betty.

Well, to tell you the truth, I immediately ran into someone who knows Gajanan, I say.

You see? I could have bet on it! You're such a knucklehead, adds my pal Ale.

So you took the savage to the pool, asks Betty, trying to imitate Monica's sarcastic tone.

We went to the pool near rue Monge, I like it a lot. Very 1930s, with the cabanas facing the pool, I find it incredibly romantic. Every time I go there I think of a Fitzgerald story. Even Gimmy whistled in admiration when he saw it. I ask him: you like it? Him: fuck, yes. Me: can't you just see Fitzgerald popping out at any minute? Him: I don't know, was he one of those Brits at the Bastille party the other night? Me: okay, let's just jump in the water.

Well, quite the beautiful illiterate beast, says Monica.

Yeah, but I wouldn't know what to say to someone like him, Betty declares.

What's there to say. Better do. (It's Nadia who says this.)

Ale chimes in: You know who he reminds me of? He reminds me of that magnificent hunk Harvey Keitel in The Piano Lesson.

I say: Yeah, like he stunk in The Bad Lieutenant, right?

Well, anyway, in The Piano Lesson . . . his character was illiterate too, but he drove that woman wild.

So what are you trying to tell me, that an ignoramus is better?

Of course not, what do I care, I'm just saying sometimes it's better to have someone who's never opened a book but makes you pee your pants laughing, you know,

Or who drives you wild in the horizontal position, says Nadia, getting straight to the point.

Monica says: Oh, my dream is a sensitive beast. A guy who thinks about things in a super simple way, you know, like primary impulses. But who knows how to be: A, sweet, B, tender, C, affectionate and sincere.

Just like Harvey Keitel, then, I go.

Aaaaaahhhhhh . . . what the hell do you know about Harvey Keitel!

Who knows what he's really like?

I read in a paper that an Italian porn star fucked him, it said that she was at some Hollywood party and she fucked De Niro first and then Harvey. De Niro was no big thing. Harvey gave it to her until she passed out.

Who knows the kind of shit she goes around talking,
Don't you badmouth my De Niro, man, that's all we need!
The one who turns me on is Willem Dafoe, you know, with
those hollow cheeks, kind of an asshole face,
　　Hey, I say, and Stallone, what about him?
　　I like Jack Nicholson,
　　Yeah, right, why not Errol Flynn.

9.

GIRLS, WE'RE AT the pool. I'm slowly going down the stairs, he jumps off the diving board, does a big cannonball, splashes water all over the place and shouts HERE I COOOOME . . . I'm swimming, pretending not to know him. He shows off his freestyle, breast stroke, butterfly, knocks aside some children in the water. Then I shout at him, hey, take it easy. He heads toward me,

Now listen to this, says Nadia.

He heads toward me, goes under water and pulls me down by the legs. I nearly had a heart attack, I wasn't expecting it. I swallowed a ton of water. He goes: hey, fathead, don't die on me now! I'm gasping for breath . . .

Listen, listen now!

. . . I say to him: fuck you, Gimmy. At which point he laughs, takes my head and pulls it toward his, really slowly. Then yours truly closes her eyes and waits to be kissed.

But instead?

Instead, bonk, he gives me a helluva headbutt.

WHAT? Instead of kissing you he laid a headbutt on you?

Yeah.

Ale says: When you swallowed all that water you must have drowned your brain.

Nadia says: You guys should have seen them, when they came to my place! And she adds: Tell them about when Julie Delpy showed up.

I continue: The funny part is that at one point Julie Delpy showed up,

Who? asks Valeria.

You know, the one who did that film with Shepard, goes Monica.

Anyway, everyone's staring at her and gaping, wow, it's her, it's her,

She's not even that great-looking, goes Monica.

No boobs and cellulite in the thighs, says Nadia.

The only good thing about her is her hair, adds Ale.

Yeah, big deal, says Valeria.

Well, anyhow, everyone's there drooling, the lifeguard's about to faint any minute. She's put her hair up and is doggy paddling real slow, to keep her tresses from getting wet. She looks around to see if anyone's watching her. Here comes Gimmy doing a crazed butterfly heading straight toward her, he's getting closer and closer . . . he crashes into her, knocks her completely aside. She's screaming hysterically, her hair's all wet, she jumps out, pissed as hell. The lifeguard goes up to Gimmy, ready to throw him out.

Tell them what Gimmy said, goes Nadia.

Gimmy starts saying, listen, you sack of shit, I'll kick your ass, you dickface, asslick. Good thing the guy couldn't understand him. I was dying of laughter. Then he calmly swims over to me.

Listen to this.

I look at him for a second, all wet, with his black hair, I mean really black, his eyes a little red, but so green. Without that bandana on his head he looked almost normal, other than the nose ring.

Now, listen to this.

Will you shut up for a second,

I hear my stomach going gurgle-gurgle, all upset.

Betty interrupts: One night after I arrived in Hong Kong I went out with this guy who'd been hitting on me on the plane. We went to a restaurant and I got an upset stomach too. I said to myself, oh god, am I really getting so excited about this guy?

But later I figured out it was because of a cold beer I drank too fast. I had the deadliest diarrhea of my life.

It's not like you couldn't spare us these details once in a while, goes Ale.

No, mine was another kind of upset, I say.

Yeah, another kind, my friend Nadia confirms.

Like what kind? asks Valeria.

The kind where I look at him and go: Gimmy, will you kiss me? He thinks it over for a second and goes: with the tongue or without? Me: however you like. Him: okay, I can do that, hold tight because we're about to take off. Let the show begin.

Omigooood!!!! goes Monica, slapping Nadia's shoulder.

Keep those mitts to yourself, goes Nadia.

What the hell did you guys do? asks Ale.

Well, we started kissing like you wouldn't believe, right there in the water, a long-ass time, my head was spinning. He says: I'm gonna knock you up right here. Then we get out of the water and start chasing each other around the showers,

Oh yeah, tell them about the showers.

He starts pinching me and giving me headbutts, he's got this thing about headbutts. I scream, like a total fool, right. We run into the women's showers and these two naked chicks start screaming and insulting us. Then came the shampoo fight, that sort of thing, you know. Okay, then we leave and that's when we ran into Gajanan's friend, this guy who studies hallucinogenic mushrooms. We had our arms around each other, Gimmy had his hand on my ass, and the guy's standing there staring at us.

Ale says: You're crazy.

Betty says: Everyone needs passion in their life.

Nadia adds: Then these two morons came to my place. And she continues: They rang the bell, I open the door, see this guy with tattoos and a nose ring, and I let out a scream. Then she pops out of her hiding place. You guys should have seen them, their hair wet, cheeks flushed, completely out of their minds. Then I touch his arm and I go: are they real? Him: what, the tattoos? Me: no, the biceps. Then I let them in and this mushbrain here goes to me, do you like Gimmy? Me: did he just escape from the circus? Her: man, something weird's happening to me, I'm crazy about him. Then I said, wait, 'cause I want to take a picture, I got the Polaroid and immortalized them.

She took a ton of pictures of me and Gimmy, I add. Then me by myself. Then me and her photographed by Gimmy, another of all of us together with the cat and the Hungarian neighbors too, like one big family.

Yeah, like the Addams family, Nadia concludes.

10.

WHAT ABOUT YOUR boyfriend? Valeria asks, didn't you think about him?

No,

What were you thinking about?

Nothing, what should I have been thinking about,

What should she have been thinking about?

I liked Gimmy.

And when exactly did you consummate? After the pool? asks Ale.

I continue: We get to my place and . . .

The telephone rings, Ale goes to answer it, then she says, pointing at me, it's for you. How did they know you were here?

I say: I did the transfert d'appel,

Transfert d'appel is a vital invention, says Monica, it's extremely useful, I'm serious.

Let me guess for what, goes Ale.

I don't know what it is, goes Valeria,

Monica explains: It's this really useful feature that forwards your calls to another number. Someone calls you and doesn't realize a thing. Get it?

More or less, goes Valeria.

Oh lord! goes Monica, then clarifies: someone calls you and they think they're calling your place. You answer but you could be anywhere, com-pree?

My friend Sandrine is on the phone sounding kind of desperate, she says, what should I do? What do you think I should do? As always, I advise: tell him to go fuck himself. Her: oh no, no I can't do it I just can't and so on and so forth.

I should tell you that my friend Sandrine is one of the few non-Italian friends I have here in Paris. I've known her for a couple of years, she's a nice, shy chick who plays the cello, kind of from another world I have to say, she lives like a nun in a large house that used to be a butcher shop, below Pigalle, it still has all the walls with the white tiles and stuff. She lives there with her dog Mimì and has a very French and very sad relationship with a married guy. He's always promising her he'll leave his wife and then obviously like hell he does.

Tonight she's telling me they were supposed to see each other, but at the last minute everything fell apart. So she's there at home with her dog Mimì tearing her heart out. Whatever. I say to her: Listen, I'm here having dinner with some of my girlfriends, do you want to drop by? We're waiting for someone else to get here. Her: no, no, I don't feel like seeing anyone. Me, muttering to myself: so much the better. Her: what? Me: nothing, never mind. What can I tell you, Sandrine? Call me back if you need anything, okay?

I return to my friends and go: Sandrine.

And Monica: Still the relationship with the marié guy?

What are you gonna do, I say.

Betty says: Women can be so self-destructive sometimes!

Ale says: Always willing to take tons of shit in hopes of finding their one True Love.

Oh, I don't do the true love thing anymore, goes Monica. I've known the true love thing makes you feel really bad ever since I turned twenty.

You're so insensitive, Betty says to her.

Damn, Ale says, Sandrine makes me think of Lucia, they were even friends for a while, you guys remember that?

Yeah, it's not like they were all that good for each other,

Ooh, Lucia had some serious gastritis attacks back then! But man, did you know she wrote fairy tales, and she's good, too, she let me read them,

She never said anything to me about this fairy tale business, goes Monica.

Who's this guy Sandrine's involved with? asks Betty.

I've never seen him, I don't know,

So what were Lucia's fairy tales about?

Man, they were so sad, they gave me a lump in my throat, there was this story about twin girls, one was bad, she swore, got angry, picked fights with everyone, never let anyone walk all over her. Then there was the other one who was really good and everyone adored her. The good one finds a husband and gets married and the bad one doesn't find anyone, and the good one goes, you see, when you're bad no one wants you . . . but when the husband locks the good one up in a tower at the end it's the bad one who frees her,

Oh god, a bit didactic, isn't it, goes Monica.

Yeah, but it was well done, there was this whole role play going on between the twins,

It doesn't take Marie-Louise von Franz to analyze it,

I knew about the fairy-tale business, but she never let me read them, she said they were a bunch of crap,

Do you remember that time at the birthday party when her guy, Jean-Claude, hung around for like three seconds and then took off, how upset she was,

She used to work her ass off, once I said to her, hey, honey, try to take care of yourself a little, and her: it's not like we're in a shampoo commercial,

She was totally defensive, you know! What could you say to her?

Listen, you guys set the table, and you, finish telling us about the savage, Ale orders.

Okay, first I'm going to pour myself another drop of wine. I continue, where did we leave off?

You went to your place after the pool, goes Valeria, who hasn't missed a word.

Here comes the good part, goes Nadia.

Allriiiight, goes Betty.

A fabulous afternoon, I say emphatic as hell to make my friends green with envy.

Okay, but were you careful, at least?

Forget it, with you guys you can never kick the level up a notch for even a second, I go.

No, really, it's nothing to joke about, you know, goes Monica.

Okay, I made him wear four condoms.

Four?

I just made that up,

Okay.

And how long did you go at it? asks Ale.

All après-midi, I go, acting important as hell.

All right, let's kick it up a notch, then, what happened? Did he give it to you like he should? Was it good? Monica insists.

Good?! It was outta this world,

How many times did you come?

I lost count.

So, the kid knows what's what, huh?

Describe,

Here's how I describe him: Kind of like a little animal, delicate, attentive und very sensitive, not to mention infinitely sweet. The kind who knows intuitively what you like and what you don't, without asking questions. He knows me like we've been fucking for twenty years.

My god! says Valeria.

If you'd been fucking for twenty years you can rest assured it wouldn't be like that, Monica declares.

I say: Then we spent the evening with Nadia and Hervé, she called me because she wanted to know how it had gone.

Always minding your own business, huh, goes Ale.

Let's open another bottle, Monica suggests.

We're on the second already, it's not even ten, Betty observes.

Come on, tonight we're going to get drunk as skunks, Monica announces with her customary finesse.

I interrupt because now I'm dying to finish my story so I go for the gold: Anyway, you gotta know that on top of everything else Gajanan was coming back the next day . . .

11.

Now we're all in motion, with Nadia and Betty setting the table, the five Afro-Belgian girls called Zap' Mama singing Nous passons de la vie à la mort and Valeria helping me drain the pasta and dump it into the giant bowl where Ale's sauce gives off an aroma that makes you drool and is guaranteed to be fattening.

My friends sniff the air and emit moans of pleasure.

Nadia says: Man, you put on weight just looking at it.

Ale says: Wait till you see the wine I got.

Dang! Corvo bianco di Casteldaccia, I've never heard of it but from the name it sounds cool!

Doesn't look like much to me.

They gave it to me as a gift.

Who gave it to you?

Ale changes the subject and goes: Let's be ladies, for once!

I don't get it, why, what the hell are we?

Speak for yourself, goes Monica.

I'm starving, your x-rated stories made me hungry,

Okay, come on, let's eat, since the pasta turned out so well, goes Ale.

For once, goes Nadia.

Finish the story about the savage, Monica orders.

First, we went to eat couscous at Omar's, says Nadia, commandeering the narrative, I brought Suspiria too.

Who's Suspiria?

My fiancé, says Nadia.

Nice foursome, says Ale.

Nadia continues: I was all decked out, I don't even know why. I had on my short black tube dress, without a bra. Even my patent leather purse. But these two looked like total bums, I mean, like, torn jeans, I was so embarrassed. Hervé didn't help either, he didn't say a word the whole evening.

Excuse me for saying so, Monica comments, but that guy is a crashing bore, you know,

Nadia continues: This moron orders four couscous royales. We had enough food for a week.

Then I got an idea, I go, hey, I have an idea! Why don't we go to Chinagora?

Where? asks Ale,

You've never been there? You really have to go! Nadia explains. Near Ivry, it's crazy, you feel like you're in China, pagodas, gardens, ponds and bridges. There's a bunch of Chinese restaurants, and a place where they do Chinese karaoke, it's full of drunk Chinese, they don't look like it, though. I mean, drunk Chinese are just like sober ones.

We take her car and go there (I'm the one talking now), we go straight upstairs, to the bar with the karaoke, we sit at a table and order Chinese beer and sake. The club is dark, in the back they're showing videos of Chinese songs, with the writing in ideograms and all that stuff. The Chinese get up from their tables, one after the other, go on stage, grab the microphone and start karaokeing. Gimmy is already drunk. He starts to laugh, he's imitating the Chinese, every so often he shouts: Far out! These chinks are too cool! He stands up and starts dancing by himself, pretending to sing in Chinese.

What an asshole! (is Betty's harsh comment.)

He takes me by the arm (I continue) and drags me to the middle of the dance floor, the Chinese see us dancing and they start dancing too. In five minutes the atmosphere of the club has completely changed. Nadia and Hervé go sit on a little sofa in the corner, they're drinking like there's no tomorrow. Gimmy and I are dancing, we're making a spectacle of ourselves, we keep kissing, he's caressing me all over, the Chinese are starting to give us dirty looks.

Now it's Nadia telling the story: I see the pirate climb onto the karaoke stage and take the microphone from this woman who's singing. He starts making up fake Chinese words, ching chang chong, crap like that, and then two beefy Manchurian guys arrive,

How do you know they were Manchurian? asks Valeria,

Come on, she just made that up, I say, taking back my story, these two bouncer types arrive, they grab him by the arms and drag him outside. Then this super-skinny guy with a gold front tooth shows up, he wants to dance with me. He was wearing this white double-breasted suit with a black shirt, he stank of whisky like you wouldn't believe, he looked like he'd escaped from the Year of the Dragon.

I could see her but she couldn't see me, Nadia says, she was standing there looking around, swearing like a truck driver, she planted an elbow into Gold Tooth's stomach, I said to myself, now he's gonna pull out a cannon and kill everyone in the club.

I say: I ran outside looking for Gimmy, he was on the ground, his T-shirt was all dirty, he had a cut over one eye. I take the Lord's name in vain every way imaginable, then I go back inside the club to look for the others, they were half asleep.

Hervé was tanked.

I go, come quick, they beat up Gimmy, he's in a bad way, he's bleeding, come outside.

Nadia says: I pull myself up, we try to drag Hervé outside, he weighs a ton, the three of us almost fell down. We get outside and park him next to the other guy.

What a pathetic scene, Monica comments, already on her second bowl of pasta.

It turned out well this time, huh, says Ale.

I'm not finished, I say, listen to this. At this point Nadia starts to scream, SHIT! SHIT! FUCKING SHIT!!!! They stole my wallet! Fuck, you guys bring me bad luck!

They stole your wallet? Valeria inquires.

Wallet complete with driver's license, credit card, and all my money.

So she took it out on me, right, I go, first an endless stream of insults, then she even slapped me in the face. With all the problems I already had. Gajanan returning from the forest, Gimmy at death's door, and my friend beating me up.

Hey, I was dead drunk, Nadia justifies herself. Anyway, you gave me a hell of a slap too.

I was drunk too, I go. And I felt like I had to puke, but I couldn't.

Charming picture, says Ale.

Yeah, then she did puke, and I even held her head,

Gross, Monica says with her mouth full.

We drag ourselves out to the parking lot, Gimmy's groaning, I thought they'd broken something, we couldn't get him into the car.

Nadia: I was saying, let's be on the lookout because I bet my ass the cops are gonna show up. And as if by magic . . .

I start toward Gimmy, I continue, but a cop comes out of nowhere and beats me to it, pounces on Gimmy, pulls him up and slams him against a car with his legs spread. I'm about to have a nervous breakdown, I open my purse to look for a tissue, but a second cop pounces on me and slams me against the hood of the car, with my face smashed down and my arm twisted behind my back. I thought I'd ended up in a Starsky and Hutch episode.

Holy shit! Betty comments incredulously, did they arrest you?

It's Nadia who continues: They fucked with us. Identification check, questions,

You guys should have heard her, I go, the two cops are giving us this hard stare, like they can kick our ass anytime they want. We felt like international criminals, at one point I started to think they were going to haul us in.

Damn, says Nadia, I sweated bullets trying to convince the gendarmes to let us go, I drove them crazy with my jabbering, I think in the end they split so they wouldn't have to listen to me anymore. One says to the other, under his breath, Qu'est-ce qu'ils sont cons ces italiens. Like, what assholes these Italians are, can you believe it?

We finally managed to get home, it must have been three, the rest of the night Gimmy kept moaning about getting beat up, his ribs were all bruised, every time I tried to touch him he yowled.

Poor thiiiinnng . . . goes Betty.

I was saying to him: shit, Gajanan comes back tomorrow. What the hell do I tell him? Him: Tell him whatever the fuck you want. He was really in a bad way! To make it short, I didn't get to sleep till morning. At ten the phone rings, a voice I must have heard somewhere before, but at the moment I can't remember where, is saying things like: airport, I'm on my way, stuff like that.

Holy mother of god, the Indian guy! says Ale.

What did you say to him? asks Valeria.

What do you think I said to him, I was going, yes, yes yes . . . then I sat straight up in bed and said: YOU'RE HERE? I jumped into a cold shower, keep in mind Gimmy was still in bed, half comatose. I felt like shit, I was nauseous, I had a headache. I tried to wake him up. He attempted to open an eye, his face was a mess. I pulled him up, tried to dress him, I was saying to him: Gimmy, Ga-Gajanan is on his way home, he'll be here soon. Gimmy I'm so freakin' sorry, but do you think you could leave? He was making incoherent sounds, and every once in a while he swore. Me: Can I call you a taxi? It ended in a shitty way, I have to say.

Will you pass me a little more pasta? asks Monica.

More? asks Betty.

It turned out okay, didn't it? Ale insists without getting any reply.

I'd like some more wine, I say.

12.

HAVE YOU SEEN The Age of Innocence? Betty asks. Your story reminds me of it,

I really don't see the connection, Monica says, in The Age of Innocence Pfeiffer is an emaciated blonde who forgoes sex with a guy because he's already engaged and has to marry another woman. Whereas this one would even jump baby jesus's bones.

Maybe you're right, says Betty.

No, Betty's right, says Nadia sticking up for her friend, because she's older than him, in the film you don't notice it so much, but that's the way it is in the book.

What's his name, that actor, kind of clueless, super uptight, always with the same expression?

Daniel Day Lewis, the one who dumped that insipid bitch Huppert?

Are you sure he was with Huppert?

Yep.

Anyway, I don't see what it has to do with my story, I go.

Well, theirs was also an impossible love, says Nadia.

But these two seem like they really got into it, right? says Ale.

No, it's because their relationship also ended badly, right?

Whatever. I've got one for you, Monica goes, another movie where you see Harvey Keitel in his underwear is coming out soon.

Wait while I write that down, goes Ale.

Have you guys seen him in Snake Eyes, when he fucks Madonna?

What, you spend your life at the movies?

Still mesmerized by the image of the naked Keitel, I go, it's true, my relationship with Gimmy really ended in a shitty way.

Go answer the phone, Monica orders.

Oh shit, what the hell's happening tonight? Ale goes, getting up from the table again. Then she turns to me and says: It's for you. It's Teresa. And in a lower voice: If she wants to sleep here, I don't have any room, got it?

Hey, Teresa, I go, how are you? Omigod, you finally came back! You're not gonna believe what happened to me! And then she jumps right into her story. Her Algerian friend Samir was letting her stay at his place, then after a while they started a relationship, a serious one. This summer she even brought him to Sicily to meet the family. This afternoon some French woman named Judith called her and asked if they could meet. To make long story short, the French woman shows up at the appointment with her belly in an advanced state of pregnancy. The child is Samir's.

Whose? asks Valeria.

The Algerian's, I go, well, actually he's half Algerian and half Tunisian.

Oh shit, goes Betty.

Plus the guy promised the French woman he'd marry her.

Uh-oh, goes Monica.

Now what? Betty wants to know.

Now Teresa's dumped him, but she feels like shit, and yet again she has no place to sleep.

Oh shit, Betty repeats.

Listen, what the hell do I tell her? I'm not leaving her on the street.

Uh-uh, goes Ale.

Of course not, goes Monica.

Can any of you guys take her in? I ask, and my friends glance around the room like they couldn't care less.

Okay, I get it, I go. I have a glass of wine and then I get an idea, I say: Hey, maybe I know where to park her, I'll send her to Sandrine's, she's got lots of space in that ex-butcher's shop.

Where? asks Monica.

At the cellist's, that way they can console each other, since they're both in a bind because of love.

Frankly, it doesn't sound like a good idea to me, goes Ale.

Then let her stay with you.

No way, go on, try Sandrine.

I dial Sandrine's number and ask if she can put up a real nice Italian friend who needs a place to stay for one night, max two. Sandrine accepts, the tone of her voice has changed, now it's all happy and carefree. She says: Yeah, sure, send her here, anyhow, I'm going out with my love. I say: Oh, he managed to free up his schedule. Her: Yes, yes, he said his wife was going out to dinner with her girlfriends. Right, I go. And a thought, too strange to entertain seriously, crosses my mind. I say: Okay, listen, Teresa will be there soon.

I return to the table saying: All taken care of,

Nadia tosses back a couple of drinks and announces: I didn't want to tell you guys this, I really didn't feel like telling you anything, but since we've come this far we might as well go all the way.

Huh? goes Ale.

You told me, Nadia, goes Betty.

Well, considering that these days you're always stuck to her like glue, goes Monica, I don't see how she could have avoided telling you.

I'm in serious trouble, Nadia confides.

Speak, Ale goes, pouring her some more wine.

I might dump Hervé.

WHAT??!! Ale goes, you're dumping that hunk Hervé?

Have you lost your mind? Valeria goes, even though she's never even seen a picture of Hervé.

I think you're doing the right thing, I say, because I know my chicken and the chicken's fiancé.

Hey, what's gotten hold of you guys? Have you all lost your minds? goes Monica.

It's your bad example, goes Betty.

Yeah, right, nice excuse,

Come on, it's the changes in the constellations, Venus is entering Scorpio, I go.

Maybe, goes Ale.

Come on, who did you meet?

No, nobody . . .

I don't believe you for a minute . . .

There's another hunk, I can smell another hunk in the vicinity. There's gotta be one, if you ask me.

Ffff, Nadia goes, annoyed. And then she adds all in one breath: I've been having an affair for quite some time. Almost a year now.

A YEAR?! You bitch, and you didn't tell us anything about it for year?!

Some friend, goes Valeria, who has known Nadia only a couple of hours.

And besides, he's not a hunk. He's Brazilian, he's got coal black eyes, a belly like this, a big butt like this, and he's really hairy. He's also really nice. Smart, and talks a blue streak,

The opposite of Suspiria, I go.

And what's the hunk's name?

Huh? Raul, his name's Raul.

What does he do? asks Monica.

He's a bioenergetics psychoanalyst, blurts Betty.

She can speak for herself, you know, I go.

Wow!! Monica goes, I've really got to hand it to you, girl. This fat-ass sounds good to me.

Where the fuck did you meet him?

At a lecture, he was giving a lecture on body expansion in bioenergy, and I went to it,

Well, if that's the case, I'll start going to lectures too.

After the lecture I went up to talk to him because he really made an impression on me,

I believe it, at 200 pounds plus, you're bound to make an impression!

Moron, I've been meaning to do something about it for a while now, I mean, I've gained too much weight,

Of course, it doesn't sound like bioenergy helped him, right?

He's not fat, he's well-rounded,

Whatever, go on,

I go up to talk to him, stand in line for forty minutes, all these women who want to know who the fuck knows what,

No men?

At one point I'm not sure whether to stay or not, it's getting late, but I hang in there, and since there's only a couple of women behind me I let them get ahead. So I'm the last one, he gives me a look, then looks at the time and goes: well, it's really late, I'm tired of talking.

Nice impression, says Monica.

Yeah, it made me feel like shit, Nadia explains, standing around like a loser all that time and then when it's my turn the guy blows me off. So, I say to him: hey, thanks a lot, first I stand in line for forty minutes . . . He looks at me again then makes a face like someone used to dealing with obsessive neurotics, manic depressives, etcetera, and says to me: okay, do you want to walk with me? I've been sitting the whole afternoon.

What a scammer, this must be a new pickup technique.

Oh come on, he was very nice and everything, but there were about two miles of wall between us. He's used to women hitting on him constantly.

A fatso like that? says Ale.

When has fat ever been a problem for men? When have men ever freaked out about a few extra pounds? (This is Monica.)

We're the only ones that dumb, goes Valeria.

That's true! Betty exclaims as if a new concept had dawned on her, opening up vast horizons.

Well, I don't know why, Nadia continues, but my knees were shaking and let's just leave it at that. Anyhow, we walk a good ways together, toward Montparnasse, it was raining like hell, but he says he wants to walk just the same. He looks at me and goes: listen, maybe you'd like to take a taxi. Like some kind of hypnotized idiot, I go, oh no, what do you mean, I love to walk in the rain, really, I always do it. Small detail, I'd just had the flu for ten days, I was sure I was gonna get sick again the next day.

Oh christ,

How did you get on an informal basis so fast?

I don't know, he asked me my name and it just seemed natural, I felt like I already knew him,

Oh no, not that, please, this business where you guys already met, maybe in a previous life, I don't want to hear it, otherwise I'll open fire, says Monica the cynic.

Uh-oh, goes Betty.

We keep walking till we get to Select and he goes: Well, we deserve a calvas, don't we?

Hell yes. At Select we start talking away, bioenergy and Brazil, and Italy, and political problems, and my personal problems. He asks me if I've ever been in therapy, and out comes my story of the five analysts plus the Buddhist guru, man, I've had more analysts than boyfriends,

Oh come on, goes Ale.

Okay, I was just saying that,

Just as long as we understand each other.

So, at one point I see people are leaving, they've already set the tables for dinner. Would you believe that I looked at the time and it was already past nine,

Well, that's not terribly late, goes Ale.

No, too bad I was supposed to be at Hervé's mother's place for dinner at eight.

Oh, what a drag,

So, I go, Raul, I have to run . . . and then I take a deep breath and shoot: b-but I w-would like to see you again. Of course we'll see each other again, he goes with a horny look in his eyes, where do you live? Me: rue Daguerre. Damn! he goes, it's destiny. Me: Um, w-what? Him: I live on rue Daguerre too.

No! Monica goes.

Yesss! Nadia goes, triumphant, his front door is practically across the street from mine. He's on the third floor, I'm on the second.

Oh shit, goes Betty.

Didn't you say you already knew this, Betty, goes Ale.

So? goes Betty, who looks to me like she's starting to get a little drunk.

And then what happened?

I quickly write my telephone number on a napkin and take off, I make it to the metro and then I'm caught in another downpour, the whole time I'm thinking: oh shit! Just that: oh shit!

So did you get sick?

No, I was too energetically charged up, I could have kissed someone with the plague and I wouldn't have caught it.

Are you going to talk like this all the time now? No, really, give us a warning, because it'd be good to know . . .

Anyway, I wasn't clear about Raul, I was excited to have found a nice, intelligent person, someone who gets it immediately if I crack a joke, who looks me in the eyes when I'm talking and tries to understand me. I mean, fuck, Hervé never understands shit, with all the crazy thoughts I have, I could never say a word to him about my subconscious. When we first met I said something to him about Jung and he goes, who, the guy with Crosby Stills and Nash? Can you believe it,

Crosby Stills Freud and Jung, I go.

Please spare us, goes Nadia.

You should've known the kind of man he was from the start, says Ale.

All smoke and no fire, Betty clarifies.

I get to Hervé's mother's house soaking wet and an hour and forty minutes late, and what's more I didn't have an excuse because I wasn't even working, Saturday is my day off. She and that idiot Hervé were glaring at me, giving me the silent treatment to make me feel like shit. I had like this atomic bomb inside me ready to explode, but the truth is that night, I really couldn't have cared less about those two. I was all charged up

from meeting Raul, I mean, he has this energy about him you
can feel, even two hours later I still felt all these vibrations,
    Of course, he's a bioenergist, I go.
    Why don't you shut up, goes Ale.

13.

MMHNN . . . So DID you see the bioenergetic guy again right away? asks Ale with her mouth full.

It's not bioenergetic, goes Betty.

We saw each other once, then I went a week without calling him. He didn't call me either. One day, though, I really felt like talking to him, so I called,

You dummy! Never go looking for them, says Ale.

You talk like my grandmother, says Monica.

I thought about him constantly, and every time I felt a surge of vitality inside, an atomic bomb of vitality. I called him at home and nobody answered, then I looked for his office number. At his office the secretary goes: the doctor is out of the country. WHAT DO YOU MEAN OUT OF THE COUNTRY??! I ask. He went to South America, the bitch goes, sounding like she's enjoying herself immensely.

Oh come on, you're just paranoid, I go.

Maybe so, but it was like pulling teeth to get information out of that bitch, damn it.

So he'd left again,

Nadia continues: I wanted to know when he was coming back, and the bitch: why, do you need an appointment? Me: well . . . not exactly an appoi— And the whore: excuse me, are you a patient? Me: well . . . not really . . . I mean, in a way . . . Her: excuse me, but are you or aren't you? Me: the hell with it, no I'm not a patient. Then I'm not authorized to give you information.

Okay, shove it up your ass, I go, in Italian. Her: pardon? Me: fuck you, and I slam down the phone.

Nice going, says Monica.

One night, note that almost a month had passed since our encounter, one night around ten, I'm at home with Hervé, he's reading a Mickey Mouse comic book, and I'm reading Lowen's Love and Orgasm,

Who's he?

Lowen, the guy who founded bioenergy, he was a student of Reich's,

I know about as much as I did before,

Forget it, don't overexert your brain or your head might burst into flames.

Okay, we're there reading and, wouldn't you know it, the phone rings?

Him.

Him.

The bioenergetic, goes Ale.

Bioenergist,

Huh?

Anyway, it was him,

Back in Paris?

Back, and he goes, Raul here, remember me? Me: damn, I mean, of course I remember you, and him: I got back from Brazil yesterday, I tried to get in touch with you before I left but you weren't home. Oh, I go, all excited but trying to restrain myself so Hervé won't get suspicious. He goes: what do you say, do you want to get together in the next few days? Me: yes, Him: When? Me: Well . . . I don't know . . . I'll call you back . . . I didn't want to make Hervé suspicious.

We already got that, go on.

Well, I was working a lot at the time, there was the new show, the one about dinosaurs, a mess. He was working all day, too, we would've only been able to see each other at night, but what the hell was I supposed to say to Hervé, I couldn't say, see ya, I'm going out with this guy tonight.

You see, girls, you're not free.

Well, it would bother me if one night Hervé went out with a female friend, just the two of them. Maybe in the afternoon, but if it was in the evening I'd get pissed, I can't help it.

I'm telling you, girls, we're really in a bad way.

That time, before the phone call, we saw each other for lunch, he had a free hour between patients, we ate a sandwich in a café full of students, at Odeon, it wasn't as nice as the evening at Select, in fact it was sort of depressing, when we left I felt so sad inside! I've gotta come up with something, I said to myself.

She told him she was coming over to my place! goes Betty, very pleased with herself.

Yeah, I fed him a line of crap. But I don't like to tell lies, I feel like a kid who has to make up stories for her parents so she can go make out, no, really, I don't like it,

Oo-kay, go on.

Plus I had some issues because I was thinking, when I tell this to my analyst he won't be happy at all. Then I didn't think about anything anymore. We saw each other again and we went to a Brazilian club, a place where they play South American music, the Canoa, it's called, in Oberkampf.

The Canoa, Valeria repeats, in Oberkampf.

As soon as we were alone in the car, close together, I wanted to kiss him so bad! He was driving and I was eating him up with my eyes. God! He made me so hot you wouldn't believe it.

Oh, man, goes Ale, pass me some more pasta, will ya?

I was telling myself, Nadia, keep cool,

What were you saying to yourself?

I was telling myself: Nadia, keep cool, stop acting like a schoolgirl, what, the first time you go out with a guy you jump on him. Man, you just don't do those things! He was talking and I could barely utter a word. All this stream of unconsciousness inside me, and then we arrived. We park, we get out, he's locking the car, his back to me, I'm behind him, I throw my arms around him, hug him tight, and he turns and goes, Ooh la la!

And you start to tango! says Ale.

We're there kissing in the middle of the street for twenty
minutes, as in till the last breath,
Doesn't he have a girlfriend?
Wait, that comes later, goes Nadia.
And you told him about Hervé?
Yeah, of course I told him.
He had no problem with it, goes Monica.
Not in the slightest, not the shadow of a problem. When we
get to the club there's a shitload of people, they tell us we have
to wait for a table. We wait for a while at the bar holding each
other the entire time. He has a way of holding me that . . . god!
I feel . . . I don't know how I feel, you know, I feel good,
Better than Hervé?
Hervé? It took me a while to figure it out, you know, I fell in
love with Hervé's looks,
Ooh, you're so superficial! Monica goes as sarcastically as
eight sarcastic Monicas.
No, really, he drove me out of my mind he's so handsome,
but he's not a sensual person. You know what I mean?
Come on, finish the story,
Wait, this is important, Hervé is handsome, so he looks like
the sexy type. But sexually he's anxious, insecure, every time we
fuck it feels like he has to perform. As if there was a camera film-
ing us, I don't know if I'm making sense. And then he's always in
a panic if I don't come quickly, I mean, it's not like it's something
you do in the blink of an eye,
You said it,
Fuck, no!
I mean, I'm really pissed now.
At who?
At Hervé. And myself. Because he was making me feel like tit.
What?
Like shit.
You said like tit.
No, I said like shit.
You said tit, didn't you all hear her say tit?

You said tit, Ale's right.

All right, go on,

Hee hee, how funny, like tit, goes Betty,

Come on, continue,

What the hell was I saying?

That at this point you're pissed as hell,

Oh, yeah, man I'm really pissed, because he'd sit there stiff as a board and after a while I didn't feel like fucking anymore. And the asshole would say to me, Nadia you're frigid, deep down you don't really like to fuck. TO ME! I mean, I was already fucking at fourteen, I was taking the pill and I had basically done my entire high school, me, who every time I see a black man on the metro I start to drool.

Far out! goes Valeria, excited, you talk so freely! she adds.

Nadia continues, all fired up: I'm the one who hitchhiked to Paris at nineteen and gave it to anything that moved for the first two years. And I don't regret it!

My god, did you take any precautions, at least? asks Betty, always worried about our physical integrity.

Listen, Snow White, without the little glove I don't even let them touch my hand, okay? I've always been free and aware (she says aware in a 1960's voice).

Hey, chill out, honey, goes Monica. We get the picture, you're really pissed,

Yeah, but deep down I'm not mad at Hervé. I'm just mad at myself, because after everything I've done in my life I ended up letting myself get tied down. I tried to change, not to look at guys on the street. I was a good girl, I wanted to be faithful. I wanted to be the little wife, to prove to myself I could be a good little wife,

Hey, you're not even married,

What's that got to do with it, these things are just part of you, like they're implanted in you from birth, in fact, in my opinion, they're written in your DNA. And at some point in life, something inside you goes off and you think, okay, up until now you've had a good time, raised some hell, barrels of it,

Of what? asks Valeria.

Huh? goes Nadia.

Barrels of what? Valeria repeats.

Forget it, goes Ale.

Nadia continues: Anyhow you've had a good time but now you need to settle down, otherwise you'll turn forty and your girlfriends are all married off, with children, a dog a cat and a house in the country and you, what the fuck are you doing, it's not like you can keep going around doing whatever you want . . .

Yes you can! goes Monica, who's also getting all worked up.

No, wait, you said something too important, you know, I go (after all, I've also read Susan Faludi's ponderous Backlash, half of that tome Sexual Personae by Camille Paglia, and even all of Feminine Mystique by the legendary Betty Friedan).

No, you can't, goes Ale, you can't because men will get pissed if you go around giving it away, if you're not there just for them. Men want a good girl, they might forgive you if you had a good time before,

In our mothers' day they wouldn't even forgive you for that,

Even if you only gave it away a couple of times, forget about it, you were in deep shit for good.

Yeah, but one morning I looked at myself in the mirror and said, Nadia, why are you playing the good little wife, all house work and fidelity? Who the fuck put that in your head?

Right,

Did you find the answer?

No.

Come on, don't be shy.

Well, I have some ideas, I'll tell you later if you feel like hearing them.

Hey, you didn't finish the story about the fat bioenergetic.

It's not bioenergetic, it's bioenergist, and he's not fat.

Yeah, yeah, yeah, he's well-rounded, okay.

14.

WELL, THAT NIGHT I took the plunge, as they say. Damn if I didn't.

Come on, don't summarize, tell us in minute detail, says Ale, dancing around on her chair to the rhythm of Lady Smith Black Mombazo.

What the hell is this music? goes Monica.

Zulu choirs, goes Ale, continuing to dance in her chair.

So, Nadia starts again, we're standing around in the club because we can't find a place to sit. Still holding each other, making out like crazy. We drink a few caipirinhas and I feel like I've already arrived at the mouth of the Amazon River.

Ooooohhh!!!!

I'm melting and I say to him, how about we leave? Him: laughing and teasing: give me a good reason to leave this nice little place. Me: I'm so wet, if we continue like this I'm gonna flood the Canoa club.

Damn, goes Ale, choking on her pasta.

Holy cow! I go.

How vulgar! The things I have to listen to, goes Monica.

We're about to go home when man-oh-man, can you believe I almost forgot where he lives?

Why, where does he live? goes Ale.

Fuck, Ale, she just told you, he lives right across the street from her, goes Betty.

Oh shit, she goes, remembering.

What if Hervé had seen you guys?

I don't know, I wasn't thinking about that. But then we get out of the car and I get all paranoid. I go, no, listen, maybe this wasn't such a good idea, maybe all that shit I said was the caipirinhas going straight to my head. And him, calm: don't worry about it, let's go have another drink, and then if you want you can go home.

Good idea, goes Ale.

What a sly horndog, that bioenergetic, goes Monica.

As soon as we get to his place and close the door he starts washing my face my neck my boobs,

What do you mean washing? asks Betty,

This guy sure is weird, goes Valeria.

What the hell do you think, I mean he was kissing me and licking me all over,

And you?

I'm bowled over. As Flaubert says about Bovary, et elle s'abandona.

Yeah, right, you hit the nail on the head with that comparison.

No, really, goes Monica, that one with Karenina, this one with Bovary, aren't you guys going a little overboard?

First he played with me until I almost died, Nadia continues, then after a lot, and I mean a loooot of fondling, we fucked.

What the hell, that's what you're supposed to do!

But if he's so fat, didn't he squash you?

I like to feel a man's weight on me, I like it a lot.

No way, if they're big I refuse to let myself be squashed,

Then what, you pass it up?

Monica says: in that case you get on top and that's the end of that.

Or doggy-style, it's doable doggy-style too, interjects Ale. And she adds: Oh shit, let me check the quiche, I'm afraid it's burnt.

What time did you go home?

That's the problem. We fell asleep. I woke at seven, I let out a scream, on top of everything else, I was supposed to be at work at eight.

Oh christ, goes Ale.

What a night, though, girls, I haven't slept that well since I was nineteen.

Try to be more composed when you speak, goes Monica.

Goddamn, Nadia repeats, with a dreamy look on her face.

And your poor fiancé? goes Monica.

Hervé . . . at first I was shitting myself, omigod, what do I tell him, oh man is he gonna be pissed, oh man he's gonna kill me, then I also thought about my analyst, what am I gonna say to Pierre, what do I tell him, he's gonna chew my ass out big time. At some point, get this, I was at the café below my place, half asleep over my coffee and croissant, a lung-trashing cigarette, and yours truly says to herself: fuck it, my life's my own and I'll do whatever the hell I want with it,

Now you're talking,

Enfin! goes my friend Nadia, I'm taking the hull by the borns, I mean, the bull by the horns, so to speak,

Yeah, you can say that all right, goes Ale.

I go to Hervé and blab everything, in minute detail.

Oh, what a mistake, what a mistake, goes Monica, never confess anything, always deny, deny everything,

Even the evidence, I add.

I saw him go pale, I thought now he's gonna faint, but he didn't. For one moment in his life he didn't think about straightening his hair. The next day I went to my analyst's and spilled my guts to him too. Only with him I had to shell out three hundred and fifty francs.

If that makes you happy, goes Ale.

I felt good, I felt strong and I wanted to be with Raul for the rest of my life. A lifetime of fucking and drinking caipirinhas.

What a prospect, man,

And maybe even pop out a few fat babies, named Pedro, Ramon, etcetera . . .

And did Raul agree?

Here comes the good part, says Betty.

Did you leave Hervé?

No, not for now, he's playing the victim, he makes me feel guilty as shit . . . and then . . . ugh . . . big discussions, he tries to talk. He says he wants to understand. I thought he would hit me, instead no, he's wracking his brain searching for dialogue: let's try to figure out together where I went wrong, where you went wrong, what was missing from our relationship,

Poor guy, goes Ale.

Me and Raul are sneaking around to see each other, just like lovers in a movie. Sex, big time. But something's changed. Something's changed since the first few times.

You're not drinking caipirinhas anymore, I suggest.

Come on, don't be a moron, she goes, the fact is the first night I really let myself go, I let myself be thoroughly manhandled and I was ecstatic.

I believe it!

Except it's not like that anymore, now I feel like I should do something, something to win him over,

Excuse me, but haven't you guys already consummated?

You really don't understand a fucking thing, do you, goes Nadia, the first night was a gratuitous thing, completely gratuitous, am I making sense? All I was thinking was that I was crazy about him, that I was dying to make love with him, and that's it. But now, now I've gotta make him fall in love with me, I've gotta know if he's serious, if there are other women in the picture, if I'm doing the right thing in dumping Hervé to be with him and so on and so forth.

And by asking yourself questions you've stopped enjoying it, goes Monica the expert.

Yeah, exactly, I've started to get uptight when we have to part, I'm sad, I feel empty as hell.

And what does fatso say?

I tried to talk to him, but he goes: I don't want you to leave your boyfriend for me.

Cold shower.

And you?

You d-don't? I go. Him: no, if you don't feel like being with him anymore then you'd be doing the right thing in dumping him, but don't dump him because you're in love with me.

Hot damn, what a man!

Well, this bioenergetic guy sounds cool to me, goes Monica.

I think he's an asshole, goes Ale, watch out Nadia, he's never gonna stay with you, he smells like a big fat rat to me.

That's what I told her too, goes Betty.

On top of that he told me he's been in another relationship for several years, with some bioenergist woman,

Oh, great! says Ale again.

But that's even better, goes Monica, what more do you want, this way he won't be after you to dump Hervé. You have Hervé and him, and he has the other bioenergist bimbo and you, what more do you want, pass me a slice of quiche, will ya?

There sure are some lucky people in this world.

Hey, I've got one for you, goes Monica with her mouth full, it's about one of my relationships, actually,

For a change.

You know I had an affair with that drummer, Frank, for a pretty long time,

Oh, we *all* know about Frank, how could we not know about Frank.

You talked our heads off about him all last winter.

Big deal, so you've got something to talk about, what are you complaining about.

I don't know who Frank is, says Valeria.

A German Swiss guy. Drummer in a rock band. Twenty-five years old, head over heels in love with this woman of loose morals, Ale summarizes.

So, at some point Frank dumped his girlfriend. I'm telling you, twenty years old, thin as a rail, big brown doe eyes and a turned-up nose. And that idiot goes and dumps her. I told him: you're completely out of your mind, you don't know what you're doing. And he, typical Swiss, goes, I don't feel like living a double life, I just don't, I love you. Well, I had a lot of fun with him, before he became a rock-and-roll version of my husband. At that point, I didn't know what to do with him anymore. I mean, you want some adventure in life, right?

That's what I say, goes Betty.

We don't want to become good little wives who bake cakes in our ovens, I mean, please.

If you ask me, you had the same effect on the bioenergetic.

But he's not even married!

He must have been, right? He must have lived with someone?

Oh, yeah, he had a wife in Brazil, and four kids.

Voilà, goes Monica, who has puffed up sixty pounds with pride for having called it right.

Wow, you really see through things, huh, says Valeria, whistling with admiration.

Hey, you know you put things in focus better than an analyst? goes Betty.

You owe me three hundred francs, I'll even give you a discount, okay, out of friendship.

Yeah but I've been feeling real bad over this, goes Nadia, getting bummed and stuff, fuck, I'm in love with that fatso!

So, did you dump Suspiria or not? I ask.

No, not yet . . . and her eyes fill with tears.

And you're still seeing Raul? asks Ale.

Yes, I . . . I can't . . . ugh, what a mess . . . and then here we go, our friend Nadia bursts into tears.

I hug her real tight and think about the time when Nadia was truly my best friend, and even though we almost never see each other anymore I think maybe she still is. Funny thing, female friendship. I give her a few strokes on the old noggin and say to her: Come on, think about when you hitchhiked to Paris . . . because that's something that immediately makes her happy.

And about when you used to give it to anything that moved, adds Betty very tactfully,

Oh shit, she goes, blowing her nose.

We need a plan, Monica proposes, come on, let's suck it up and finish the quiche, like good girls.

At least it's not plasticky like the last time, I go.

No, it's only a little burned, goes Betty.

15.

SHOULD WE BREAK out the ice cream? Ale asks.

What kind did you get? Monica asks.

Häagen-Dazs, malaga and hazelnut.

Yuck, Nordic ice cream! says Betty, like some kind of know-it-all. How could you do such a thing? The best ice cream in the world is Italian!

Well excuse me, says Nadia, pissed, because she is precisely the kind of person who can't stand that kind of comment.

Ladies! goes Monica, throwing her hands in the air. We're in Paris! All of us Italians hang out together, we always speak Italian, we eat Italian food . . . Give me a break!

But we hook up with foreigners, goes Nadia.

We've created a sort of Little Italy.

Yeah, well, I think the advantage of living abroad is that you can choose the Italians you want to hang with, but in Italy you have to deal with the whole bunch,

Plus Italian television! goes Nadia.

Shut up, you got cable just to watch the Italian evening news, blurts Betty.

So? goes Nadia.

Ooh, bad sign, we're on the verge of the immigrant syndrome. We'll do anything to feel a little closer to the fatherland, even watch the TG1 news, Monica concludes, opening the ice cream.

Anyway, let's not get ourselves down thinking about depressing things, let's eat the ice cream and forget about it, I declare.

So, how do you do it? Nadia asks Monica, returning to the topic close to her heart.

Huh? asks Monica.

I mean, insists Nadia, do you really enjoy your extramar—

No, uh-uh, don't say that word because I hate it.

Extra what?

Sh, I go, when she gets pissed she's terrible.

No, seriously, how the hell do you do it?

Don't you ever fall in love?

Always, I always fall in love, every single time.

And you never think about leaving Paul?

If you ask me, you're a lot like Madame Bovary, goes Ale.

Madame Bovary c'est toi! exclaims Monica, irritated.

Well, I am faithful, Ale declares. I just can't cheat, I can't help it. I was raised that way, and there's not a damn thing I can do about it.

We were all raised that way, honey. But how about getting past that and taking a couple of baby steps on your own, know what I mean?

Know what I mean? Betty repeats.

You go to hell, goes Ale.

Why? goes Betty, turning beet red again.

No, no, I . . . I just can't do it. I mean, the minute I get the urge to cheat on someone it's a sign that things aren't going so well anymore, it's a sign that something has ended. Maybe I don't want to admit it to myself, but that's the way it is, says Ale.

Oh, it's always the same story, goes Monica.

But do you love your husband? asks Nadia.

Yes, I do, I'm fond of him, I think he's sweet. When he's in a good mood he's actually nice, and I like the way he fucks. Of course variation isn't his strong suit, but I like it. I fall for the guys I have affairs with too, but I definitely don't want to end my marriage or run off to Mexico with my lover like they do in the soaps, because I know that every lover who turns into a husband becomes a husband.

I'll have to write that down, goes Nadia.

Monica eats some more ice cream and continues: Plus, when you're alone it's such a pain, one way or the other you're always on the hunt for someone who wants to get serious, always afraid the guy just wants to have fun, it's eating you up inside, a thousand useless questions. My way, the domestic tranquility side is all taken care of, and the wild sex side, too.

You kill me, goes Valeria. You're so cool, Monica!

Take it easy, otherwise it'll go to her head, I go.

In the beginning I did try, Monica continues, what do you think. I mean, to be a wife. Not the home-loving, church-going type, no, but still going out, doing my own thing. Minus the affairs. Well, it didn't work, girls, I was bored, and he was getting bored being with a bored woman.

And then?

Then I said to myself, Moneek old girl, what's wrong with you? What is it about you that makes you different from other wives? Why are you bored and the others aren't?

And what did you tell yourself? asks Ale.

What did I tell myself? Girls, I looked around, I talked with other women, and it's not like the ever-faithful were oozing joy and fulfillment from every pore. So I found an answer, at least an answer that works for me. I told myself, honey, nothing's wrong with you, it's the high-fidelity marriage that doesn't work!

Great, goes Nadia.

Too easy, goes Ale.

You talk like a man, goes Betty.

Why should I talk like a woman?

Of course, men have kept for themselves everything that doesn't involve paranoia and left us the worst, I go, sounding kind of like Betty Friedan in her early days.

You're all sitting there asking yourselves how a relationship should work, Monica continues, how you should act to make it work well, but you've never thought about acting in a way that makes your life work? Always thinking about relationships, what do I do to get him, what do I do to keep him, what do I do to make him dump the other woman. Hasn't it ever occurred to you to ask yourselves, what can I do to make myself happy? To enjoy life to the max without sitting around beating myself up?

No, says Betty.

Hey, Moneek, chapeau, goes Nadia.

No, seriously, you kind of come across like a flake, but damn, you've really got your shit together! I go.

Thanks a bunch, she goes.

Hey, Simone de Beauvoir's got nothing on you, goes Ale, attempting to play the irony card, but I'd say she's lost the hand and she knows it.

I'm gonna say one more thing and then I'll drop it. I've learned that when I live my way, without following other people's rules, without trying to do what people generally think is right, or what everyone else does, things go really well, and I feel great!

Here, have some more wine, I say.

Let's make a toast! goes Valeria.

To not following the rules, goes Betty.

Oh Lord, goes Ale.

No, wait a minute, what about Paul? Don't you ever think about him? About whether he's feeling bad? Don't you give a damn about hurting him?

I told you, knucklehead, Paul is a lot happier with me when I'm happy. And besides, I think fessing up is just a way to relieve your own guilty conscience.

And a cruel way, to boot.

Out of sight, out of mind, Valeria pronounces.

That's so hypocritical, says Nadia.

Call it whatever the fuck you want, goes Monica, keep your cystitis and go on getting fleeced by your shrink.

What's cystitis got to do with it? goes Valeria.

No, I think it's something else, too, goes Ale. What I think is you don't work, you don't do a fucking thing all day, so you get bored and then you go around looking to get laid.

Better going around looking to get laid than working, I go.

She's right, goes Monica.

Thanks, I go.

No, really, I've never understood the bullshit people say about work. That women should find fulfillment in work, that if you work you have your own identity . . . Who's ever been fulfilled from work?

Eleonora Duse, Virginia Woolf,

By work I mean doing something you don't give a damn about,

Look, if you ask me it's not like that for men either.

They teach you that working makes you forget your paranoias, thanks a lot, you lose your mind, and you forget everything.

I don't work, adds Monica, but I walk in the park, I go to the movies, the theater, I read, I bullshit with my girlfriends, I get laid . . . and frankly, I've never felt so good!

Great, goes Ale.

No, wait, I get what she's saying,

Like, when I have sex with a guy it always feels like I have to choose between giving myself up or giving up a fuck. In the end I usually give myself up.

It must have something to do with that. Like, in my case I think, did I do the right thing, did I say the right thing? Am I the type of woman he'd like? And then little by little I end up trying to change myself accordingly,

The thing is, for me, I'm too hungry for love to let me be myself. That's why I have to choose between being myself or being loved.

Bullshit.

No, really, it's true.

Take you, Ale, goes Monica, since you started going with Gianni you've put on a ton of weight, you've started cooking and you're behind in your exams at the university.

The doorbell, goes Nadia.

Huh? goes Ale.

Someone's ringing the doorbell.

Ale gets up and says: Hey, what do you want to bet Lucia is here, go open the door, I have to pee, I can't hold it anymore.

Monica gets up and goes to the door.

16.

OH NO! GOES Betty,

We hear shouting, a commotion, Nadia gets up and goes to the door too. She yells: The kraut is back and on the offensive again.

The scene has moved to the apartment door. There's a tall, blonde woman with pigtails, all red in the face. She's wearing a down vest over a jogging suit, and she proclaims: That whore!

Monica says: Who's a whore?

The German woman insists: Where's your whore friend?

I think she's referring to Ale, goes Nadia.

Listen, calm down a minute, goes Monica.

What the fuck do you want, says the German and gives Monica a big shove. Where is she hiding?

What do you want? goes Ale from inside the john.

The woman rushes to the john, opens the door and sees Ale sitting on the pot. Oh no, not in the john, please, she goes, not here. The German grabs her by the shirt and says: Come out and fight. Hey, calm down, says Ale, who has been yanked off the pot with her underpants half-way down and is now engaged in hand-to-hand combat with the Teuton.

We try to separate them, Monica catches another big shove, me a mean elbow in the eye.

Are you guys crazy?! shouts Valeria.

Let's talk a minute, ma'am, says Betty.

I not talk, I kill, the German retorts. I break everything, why you take my man away? Where you hide him?

Listen, let's clear up this nonsense once and for all, it's not like Gianni's a baby and I'm not hiding anyone. And besides, he's not your man anymore. It just so happens he's mine now! says Ale, still wrestling. With these words both of them hit the floor and we witness a fine example of no-holds-barred freestyle fighting,

What a show, goes Monica,

Come on, let's do something, I go.

No way, I don't want to get hit again, says Monica,

Dumb shits, says Nadia, throwing herself into the fray.

After they've beaten the hell out each other, Nadia almost manages to separate them.

Help me, she yells to Betty, and Betty lunges into the fray with a flight attendant's characteristic sense of fair play,

Let's talk, says Ale.

Ow, this woman's killing me, goes Betty. She pulls herself up and goes: Oh God, I feel sick, Oh God, I'm dying.

Oh Christ, says Monica.

Now what the fuck is wrong with you, goes Ale.

Betty is as white as a sheet. Monica goes: What's the matter with you, come on, sit down a minute, drink a glass of water . . .

No, no, goes Betty. Oh God, it hurts, she says, holding her belly.

Dammit, what the fuck's the matter with you? Ale says again.

What do you want, you think if you kill her he'll come back to you? He's not coming back, goes Monica, who has managed to get the German to sit down.

Here, have some wine, goes Nadia.

Listen, we were all just talking about cheating . . . says Monica.

Shut up! goes Nadia, silencing her with a dirty look.

Cheating????!!! says the German, and off she goes again, pouncing on Ale like a wild beast.

Come on, cut it out you guys, goes Betty, I'm feeling sick.

What's the matter? Will you please tell us what's wrong? says Nadia.

I didn't take anything from you, goes Ale. He told me it was already over between you, that you never had sex, that you only gave it to him once every two or three months!

That bastard! shouts the Teuton. And he owes me ninety thousand francs too!

Is it true you only had sex every two months? asks Monica.

Every day! We made love every day! After eleven years together!

Oh, says Ale, making a face like someone who's just eaten a turd.

Ooooowww, goes Betty, holding her belly.

All alike you Italians! All same! shouts the kraut. And she adds: But I want my money!

I make him shit it out!

Hey, take it easy with the racism, goes Monica.

Racism my ass, she shouts, pronouncing the swear words extremely well. All scoundrels, liars, cheats. He owes me ninety thousand francs. And the money for the kids. Scoundrel, cheat.

How much is ninety thousand francs? asks Ale.

Thirty million lire, more or less. goes Monica.

The German has stopped to catch her breath and then she adds: And the women, all whores, she shouts and lunges for the umpteenth time at our friend Ale. It takes three of us to pull her off.

Listen, we don't know what to tell you. Anyway, if he's a lying insincere cheat, aren't you better off without him?

She's quiet for a second and then starts to cry. Betty starts to cry too.

Oh no! goes Nadia.

Here, drink some white Corvo, go on, goes Ale.

You must be pretty worn out, huh, I go to Betty.

The German glugs two full glasses and calms down.

Wouldn't you like some eggplant pasta? It's really good, you know.

Have you eaten anything yet? asks Ale.

I have not ate for a month!

Whoa, who are you, Siddhartha? asks Monica.

Shut up, stupid, says Nadia.

Someone's ringing the doorbell again,

Hey, are we in a Feydau play or something?

This time the shouting we hear is more festive: Hey, where the hell have you been, hey, what the hell have you got on!!

A woman I'm sure I know, but I can't remember from where or when, walks in. Me, Monica, Nadia, all of us are just sitting there gaping. Except for the kraut, who's silent, staring at her shoes.

Suddenly Monica screams: NO!! LUCIAAAAAA, IS THAT YOUUUU!!!???

Nadia repeats: LUCIAAAA, WHAT DID YOU DO TO YOUR HAAAAIR!!??

And your clothes! What did you do with your nice little outfits!?

So yes, the woman before us is none other than Lucia, who disappeared last July and was given up for lost. What has also disappeared are her tailored suits, now she's wearing a pair of jeans, torn at the knees, and a green, yellow and red tank—the familiar colors of Jamaica—without a bra. She's cut her hair Sinead O'Connor-style, but picture a Sinead who hasn't shaved in a month and looks like she stuck her head in bleach. What I'm trying to say is that the color is bright yellow, almost golden.

I can't believe it, goes Nadia,

Did you escape from the zoo? goes Monica.

Did the savages get you? goes Ale.

Who's she? asks Lucia, indicating the German.

She's Gianni's ex, says Ale.

I thought so, goes Lucia,

Come on, tell us everything, spill it,

Good god, what the hell have you done to your hair,

It was so beautiful!

What do you mean beautiful, she looked like a nun.

What's the matter, Betty? Are you sick? asks Lucia.

She got sick while these two were beating each other up.

So? Where the hell were you? goes Nadia.

Can I stay here at your place for a few days? Lucia asks Ale.

Oh, sure, maybe even with our friend Beate.

The German's name is Beate? asks Valeria.

Yeah, the perfect name, huh,

Lucia O'Connor tosses back half a glass of grappa and announces: I was in Berlin.

So what got into you?

I ran off with Ralph.

And who the fuck would this Ralph be?

Can I have something to eat? Then I'll tell you.

Did you know that Jean-Claude was really worried? goes Ale.

He called me three thousand times, goes Monica.

Slow down, I want to know everything from the beginning, I go.

17.

Stuffing herself with pasta, the transformed Lucia is about to begin her story.

Nadia asks: Don't you have gastritis anymore?

Lucia shakes her head and, continuing to eat, goes: Mmhnn . . . no,

So? I prompt.

Do you guys remember Philippe, that writer I liked?

Here we go again with that pompous ass, I go. I realize it would have been better if I had kept my mouth shut. I say: Pardon.

Lucia goes: No problem, you were right about him,

He is a pompous ass?

And other things besides.

Such as?

He doesn't like women.

No! Nadia goes.

I could have sworn it, I go.

Wow, you know everything, Betty says to me.

Drop it, Betty, goes Ale.

Well, one night he invites me to his place and there were these guys there, weird types, you know the kind that dress in black leather, like bikers? Studs, bandanas on their heads, really weird,

Were you in a Fassbinder film or something?

Does the pompous ass have a nice place?

You should see it! Completely done in deco style.

Oh, so he must sell well, says Valeria.

Like all pompous asses, the more pompous they are, the better they sell. That's the way it works, I go.

Hey, you're not jealous, are you, goes Monica, pleased as punch.

No, really, they were weird. There were only two women, me and this chick dressed just like them. Philippe didn't even look at me the whole evening, I'm sitting there in a corner with a glass in my hand like an idiot. Every once in a while, I try to get him to notice me, but nothing, the whole time he was glued to this guy, who really did look like he came out of a Fassbinder film. Big as a house, square jaw, leather pants with a really low-cut tank, chest hair on display, and a black cap on his head.

Man, how come you never call us when you go to these parties, says Monica.

Trust me, you wouldn't have had a good time either, she goes.

Who were they, anyway?

Americans, Californians . . . Germans, I don't know. I was totally blown away when Philippe takes the hulk and disappears into the bedroom.

Oh dear.

Can you believe that guy, so refined and all,

So he's a fag all right!

I could have bet my ass on it, I repeat.

But why didn't he ever tell you? I mean, if he'd said something before . . .

Well, for me it would have been a shock all the same.

Wouldn't you know it, goes Monica.

And you ran off because of that? asks Betty.

Listen to this. I'm sitting there feeling like shit, still in my corner,

Couldn't you have left?

I felt like I was paralyzed,

Oh Lord,

Luckily there was this nice guy.

Handsome?

Not bad, a big guy, also covered with studs, with really long, straight hair, jet black,

Who was he, Cochise?

We started chatting. Beneath that badass exterior was a gentle soul. He had a really beautiful smile, goes Lucia, looking lovely again and carried away by the memory.

Wait a second, was he American?

Uh-uh, he's German, from Hamburg.

Hamburg? asks Beate. Maybe I know.

No! Not the phone again! I'm gonna take it off the hook, says Ale. She talks in a low voice for a while, then says: NO! I ask: What's happening now? Ale goes: Come here, it's for you, Teresa again.

I wouldn't want to get up from the table for anything in the world, but even so, I get up and say to Teresa: Are you at Sandrine's? All settled in? She says: hey, your friend Sandrine is real nice, you know?

Me: yeah, that's true. When she's not depressed she's nice.

Her apartment's not too shabby either,

Me: Yeah, I know. It used to be a butcher shop. Anyway, if you're all right I'll let you go, Teresa, because Lucia is here and . . .

Listen, girl, goes Teresa, I don't know how to tell you this . . .

What? I go.

Well, since Sandrine's out, I've been wondering whether I should mind my own business, then I decided it was better not to.

What happened, I go, worried.

Well, this guy came to pick her up, the one she's having the affair with . . .

Does that bother you?

Yeah, me, right . . . no, it's just that, listen, it's a funny thing, your friend who works in TV, what's her name, Nadia, is she there with you guys?

Yeah, we're all here at Ale's.

You're at Ale's place?

Ye-es.

But I called your number, she goes.

Look, I have call forwarding, I go, getting antsy. What did you want to tell me? What does N—

Shh, don't let anyone know I'm talking about her . . .

What the fuck are you talking about, Tere—

Okay, you need to find out if that guy, her boyfriend, the cute one, has a twin brother.

WHAT??!! I go.

Yeah, the guy, I mean, the guy that came to pick up Sandrine, look, either it's Nadia's boyfriend or it's his twin brother.

Filthy, disgusting piece of shit! I interject.

What is it, what's going on? goes Nadia.

No, nothing, Teresa's problems.

Well, listen, Teresa, I'll think of something and then I'll call you back. Did he recognize you?

I don't think so, after all, I must've only seen him a couple of times, I think. But I never forget a face, I'm a great physiomnogist! Everybody tells me so.

Physiognomist, I correct her, and then I get back to my friends because Lucia is going on with her story.

She says: I was depressed, I'd been drinking, you all know I never do. I felt like I was going to throw up. In short: I started telling him my life story.

Who? I ask.

Ralph, the German guy. I spilled my guts, I told him about my boyfriend and how he studies prison systems,

He studies what? asks Beate.

He studies prison inmates, the people who sit in the slammer, right? goes Monica.

Then I told him about my longtime crush on Philippe. Oh, but Philippe isn't interested in women, didn't you know that? goes this guy Ralph, caressing my face and drying my tears. Then he takes off my glasses and . . . and he lets my hair down,

Like in the movies! goes Nadia.

He starts gazing into my eyes. You have very sweet eyes, he goes.

Woww . . . goes Ale.

I was so embarrassed! adds the shy Lucia.

What language were you guys speaking?

Italian, he knows Italy well, he's done a lot of political work there.

Political work? What is he, a diplomat?

No, *another* type of politics, get it?

Omigod! Is he a skinhead?

She just told you he has long hair!

The opposite.

Okay, forget it, she got stuck with an international terrorist.

He's not a terrorist.

Listen, angel face, I go, can't you for once in your life find a normal guy, hmm? Either it's some big-time professor who only thinks about his work, a vile, phony fag, or an international wacko?

My friend Lucia shrugs.

Maybe it's her karma, says Nadia,

What sign are you? asks Beate.

Scorpio with loser rising, goes Monica.

C'mon c'mon, tell us the rest.

German men much muuuch better than Italian, goes Beate.

Hey, Beate, you want some more wine?

Oh god, I'm gonna end up having to carry her home on my back, goes Ale.

So anyway, Lucia continues, I'm there feeling all bummed over Philippe, not to mention my boyfriend, who never goes to parties with me, who's always keeping to himself, and I thought, it can't go on like this.

So your boyfriend is a bore, goes Beate, who is beginning to participate in the conversation.

Yeah, like the majority of French men, says Monica.

So why did you hook up with him? asks Valeria.

It's true, French men are almost always boring, confirms Betty.

And Italians they big scammers, Beate hastens to add.

Anyway, we're there talking and drinking, and he goes, listen let's get out of this place, you shouldn't be here, you're humiliating yourself,

Hey, come on, let's not be so melodramatic.

So we leave, and . . . well, what the hell, I say to myself, and the next thing you know I find myself with this half stranger in a hotel room,

WHAT?

Near Cherche Midi somewhere. At least, I think,

Hold on, did I understand you right? In a hotel room?

Uh-huh.

Can you believe this girl?

And . . . did you consummate?

It was the most wonderful night of my life, it was . . .

Magical? I suggest.

Oh, why do we women always have to refer to getting some as magic! says Monica.

Shut up you insensitive bitch, goes Nadia.

Well, at first, he couldn't even do it,

German men, huh? says Monica to Beate.

Wait, you don't think this guy was a fag too?

No, no way.

No way, Ale mocks her,

He was there with some friends, they were just friends . . . We held each other and talked for a long time. Part two of the story of our lives. I told him things I'd never told Jean-Claude. I told him more that night than I'd told Jean-Claude in five years.

Great,

So why didn't you ever talk to the sociologist?

Have you ever tried to talk to someone who doesn't show the slightest interest in your innermost feelings? says Lucia.

Every day, goes Nadia.

So, what, you guys just spilled your guts to each other?

We talk and talk, and the next thing you know he gets a hardon,

Whoa, where did all this come from? says Monica.

18.

HEY, LET'S OPEN the window a little, you can't breathe in here, Ale suggests.

When are you going to pull out the surprise? asks Monica.

After we've gotten some air, says Nadia.

What's the surprise?

Come on, tell,

No, uh-uh . . . Okay, herb-flavored grappa.

GOOD HERB?

Real good, homegrown, Nadia goes.

I'm busy opening the bottle that will deal us the final blow, and I say: I want to hear how the story ends.

Me too, says Beate, who looks like she's becoming a part of our crazy crew.

Lucia is digging into the pasta, she must be really hungry, but she continues: Then we fell asleep. At one point I wake up and it's after four, omigod, what am I going to tell Jean-Claude now?

Come on, all he thinks about is prisoners anyway!

Yeah, drop it.

So, I quickly get dressed and go out into the street to look for a taxi, but I'll be damned if a single one passes. Ralph followed me out, he comes up to me and goes: I'll go with you. We walked the whole way hand in hand, leisurely, like I really didn't give a damn how late it was.

I want some grappa, goes Valeria.

We say goodbye in front of my building. Another twenty

minutes of kissing, I'm starting to get nervous, he goes, I'm leaving tomorrow, I want to see you again before I go. I say, no, please, listen, it's been great but it's better to end it now.

What a spazz! screams Monica.

Girl, we still have a lot to teach you.

The next morning was Sunday, I wake really late,

What about Jean-Claude? Didn't he suspect anything?

Are you kidding? When I got home he was sleeping like a log, he didn't realize a thing.

Lucky you, you've got a man who's completely out to lunch, goes Monica.

Yeah, well, Paul deserves a golden palm, too, for best performance as the most cheated-on man of the century,

Hey, don't diss my Paul,

So, Sunday morning I take my shopping cart and go to the organic market on boulevard Raspail,

I can't stand that place, all those pseudo-alternative-lifestyle types, bearded young fathers with kids hanging on their backs . . . the people there make me want to puke.

I belief they have excellent stuff, says Beate.

So, I looked like a bum, with my espadrilles, a pair of bermudas and a T-shirt with the Franprix Supermarket logo on it.

How come you didn't have one of your usual pastel poop-colored suits on? asks Monica.

God, I was completely out of it . . .

Wow, this grappa very good, says Beate.

I do my shopping and then I go sit in a café nearby, I needed to get my thoughts together. I'm there with my lemon tea, I eat my little organic carrot focaccia from the market . . .

Yuck, how gross,

I'm gonna throw up, goes Betty.

Oh god, Betty, what's wrong with you, goes Ale.

I don't like the way she looks at all, says Monica.

I'm there in the café, Lucia continues, staring out at the street, placid bovine style. I was still thinking about the night before, I was thinking about Ralph, about his arms and his smell, saying to myself, I wonder where he is now, if he's already left he could be there . . . who knows . . . and while I'm all wrapped up in my thoughts, coup de théâtre, I see a black leather jacket go by, out in the street, black hair blowing back, all on a huge, red bike.

NO! goes Ale.

Shit! goes Monica.

Get out! I go.

Was it the German? asks Monica, draining her grappa and letting loose an elegant belch.

Him. I let out a scream, everyone in the café turns to look at me. I get up, run outside waving my arms and shouting: Ralph! Ralph! But he doesn't hear me. I run across the street and nearly get run over by a van carrying organic vegetables. I'm standing there in the middle of traffic, my arms hanging at my sides, thinking I must be hallucinating, maybe I'm going crazy. I go back across the street, return to my table,

After that nice spectacle, my friend Ale comments.

I had just sat back down when . . .

He drove by again! goes Nadia.

This time I started shouting like a lunatic, he turned and finally saw me. He drops the motorcycle in a heap in the middle of the street. Cars are honking behind him, he raises his middle finger at them, like this.

Quelle finesse! the extremely refined Monica comments.

He comes up to me and we start kissing right there, holding each other real tight. He goes, hi, I've been waiting outside your building since eight this morning.

Omigod, how romantic! screams Valeria.

See how nice German men! says Beate.

I'm so happy, says Lucia, I feel like I'm dreaming, I try to say something but as soon as I open my mouth he kisses me again. Then he takes me by the hand and goes: come on I want to show you something. Me: wh-what?

What? asks Monica, who after the grappa is attacking the ice cream again.

Lucia says: His motorcycle.

Ale says: I don't trust guys who ride bikes.

Yeah, right, like there aren't any sons of bitches going around on foot, right, goes Betty.

Or in cars, Nadia adds.

Ralph shows me the motorcycle and says: do you know what this is? Me: a motorcycle. Him: wrong! This isn't a motorcycle. This is a thoroughbred horse. And it'll take us far away from here.

What kind of bike was it? asks Monica.

I don't know, a Suzuki, huge, it went 170 miles per hour, I was scared just looking at it.

You are one lucky-ass woman, Luci, goes Nadia.

Monica says: Quiet.

Lucia continues: I go, excuse me, how do you mean, far away? He kisses me again and goes: get on, we're leaving. WHAT DO YOU MEAN LEAVING!? I go, about to have a heart attack. Say goodbye to the professor and let's get out of this place, he adds, we're made for each other.

Omigod . . . Ale comments, concerned.

I was really freaked out, I go: listen Ralph, I gotta talk to you. We've had a nice fling. Him: you might even say it was out of this world. Me: u, yeah, I agree, but I'm . . . I'm a w-woman . . . And all this time I thought you were a transvestite, he goes.

I like this Ralph, I go.

Lucia continues: And be-besides I have an obligation to Jean-Claude . . . I can't just dump him like this . . . Ralph: I guess not, huh!

Monica says: You're kind of a jerk too, though. First, this big deal about the magic night and stuff, and then you pull out this obligation to Jean-Claude.

Beate adds: Who, among other things, doesn't even notice if you spend night out.

And then? asks Ale.

He got pissed, punched the seat of the motorcycle and said: fuck it, I'm leaving. I felt like crying, he takes me in his arms once more and starts kissing me again à la gone with the wind.

Then he looks me in the eyes and goes: so? Me: I'm coming with you, Ralph.

Omigoooooooodd . . . Ale says, come on, pass me the grappa.

He goes: Get on. Me: I can't just leave, dressed like this, in my bermudas, I have to get some things, plus I have to tell Jean-Claude. Him: okay, let's say that if you don't come back in half an hour I'll leave.

Oh god, now I'm all worked up too, I go. Is there any ice cream left?

19.

I TRUDGE HOME, Lucia continues, my head is spinning. I open the door and scream in a strangled voice: JEAN-CLAUUUUDE . . . ARE YOU HEEEEERE???! Silence. My legs are shaking, I'm thinking: Maybe I'll just write him a letter. Then I think: yeah, but what do I write: dear Jean-Claude, I wanted to tell you I'm leaving with my biker lover, we'll drive slow, don't worry.

And have a good vacation, Nadia suggests.

Then I say to myself, no, it's better if I don't write him anything, I'll just leave, and then I'll call him tonight.

Yeah, that way he'll definitely feel better, says Monica.

I start getting some clothes together, a skirt, a linen jacket, a silk shirt . . .

Yeah, the perfect outfits for running off on a motorcycle.

A necklace, the hairdryer, some tampons . . . Lucia says.

It's okay if you don't give us the complete list,

Oh, and a book of poetry by Silvia Plath, adds Lucia.

Of course, that's indispensable when you're taking off with your lover,

I also do a few yoga postures, to relax,

You were freaking out, weren't you, says Betty,

Mind your own business, goes Nadia.

That's when I notice my legs (it's still Lucia talking),

What's wrong with your legs?

They were really hairy. I forget the yoga and head to the

bathroom to look for the Veet. I can't find it. I check the time and fifteen minutes have already passed.

Veet doesn't work very well, anyway, says Monica.

Then I think I should probably take some heavy sweaters if I'm going to be riding on a motorcycle, and maybe even some socks, and my tennis shoes.

Yeah, that might be better than a nice little linen skirt,

I stuff everything in my bag, which is overflowing. I empty everything out on the bed again, then panic hits me. I decide to get in lotus pose and breathe. I'm sitting there with my legs crossed when I hear the key slide into the lock.

Oh shit, goes Ale.

Jean-Claude? I ask.

It's him alright, says Lucia. He looks around, sees the mess on the bed. Then he sees me sitting on the floor like a lunatic, and goes: are you cleaning or meditating?

I really can't stand that guy, goes Monica.

I get up, throw my arms around him, and go: Jean-Clauuuude . . . and I start to cry,

It's a habit then,

He goes: hey, careful! Don't squeeze me so tight. Then this anger comes over me . . . I take a breath and say: I'm leaving. Him: are you going to the movies? If you like I'll go with you, I really don't feel like working today . . . I take another deep breath and shoot, all at once: Jean-Claude, I have a lover, I'm leaving with him.

HOLY FUCK! goes Nadia,

And him?

He says: okay, I get it, you want to go by yourself. Listen, I've invited a few people over for dinner tonight, okay, I hope you went to the organic market this morning . . .

Good god, he should be killed, Monica comments.

20.

GODDAMN! SAYS ALE. You sure had guts.

I couldn't have done it, says Nadia.

Lucia says: When I left the apartment I was a wreck. A voice inside me was saying: you'll come to a bad end. You're headed down the wrong path. You'll wind up like Effi Briest, or Hester Prynne, maybe even Tess.

You read too much, goes Nadia.

Who are they? The British girls you work with? asks Betty.

You're so ignorant, Betty, goes Ale. And she adds: Hester Prynne's a character from a Lynch film, right?

That's right, Tess is the one who ended up hanged, I go.

What? asks Nadia.

Lucia shakes her golden-yellow head and continues: Why do stories about adulterous women always have a shitty ending?

It's simple, honey, it's because men are the ones telling them, declares Monica.

Hey, I never thought about that! says Ale.

Lucia goes on: Then I looked at the time and realized the half hour Ralph gave me was long passed. I said to myself, what am I gonna do if he's already gone?

Well, you could have always gone back to the sociologist and told him you were playing a prank on him, goes Ale.

Or that you didn't like the movie, Nadia suggests.

Anyway, I'm on boulevard Raspail once again with my bag. I don't see Ralph. I try to breathe deeply. A motorcycle pulls up.

Like in the movies, says Nadia, I can't believe it!

Except it wasn't him. I start to get pissed off, I tell myself: shit, I drop everything for him, and the asshole can't even wait an extra ten minutes! I grab my bag again and head toward the metro. I have no idea where to go, but I'm not going home.

Good for you! goes Beate approvingly.

So I'm walking, when someone cuts me off. I scream: MOTHERFUCKER!

Since when did you start being so vulgar?

Was it him?

He nearly ran me over. Then he takes off, turns around and heads right at me.

They've opened the cages, says Monica.

I say: where the hell were you? Him: you really came! Me: here I am. Him: you did it, would've ever thought! Get on. I put the bag in back and get on.

NOOOOOOO!!! Ale goes.

So you dumped Jean-Claude! says Betty.

How did you feel? asks Monica.

On the one hand total panic, on the other I felt really strong inside, I didn't give a damn about anything, I was really happy I was doing something so crazy after being a good girl for so long.

I take another slug of grappa, light myself a lung-trashing cigarette and say: Tell us about the road trip.

Lucia runs a hand through what's left of her hair and starts again: We went to the Midi, in Provence, we drove almost five hours straight, stopping only to get gas and pee.

You make me want to ride a motorcycle again, you know, I haven't been on a bike in ages, goes Nadia.

Come on, be quiet, suck down some more of granny's grappa, says Ale.

So you rode around Provence? asks Betty with a worldly-drunk air.

The heat was awful, says Lucia. I say to Ralph: it's hot as hell, and he goes:better hot than rainy. Once we got to Avignon, we ran into an incredible storm. I was so scared, storms have always terrified me.

Lordy!

Then where did you guys go?

Oh, we traveled around a lot. For example, we went to Arles, it was really beautiful there. We found this boarding house, it was so romantic! Right next to the cathedral, on a little medieval street . . . We walk in and the man at the desk, a bald guy with porcine eyes looks us up and down. Ralph goes: you have a problem? And the man: pardon? You have a problem? He says he wants to be paid upfront. Ralph pulls out a wad of money from the inside pocket of his jacket. Dollars, in fact. My eyes pop out of my head, then I try to compose myself, so I don't make the hotel guy suspicious. Ralph lifts me in his arms and we go up the stairs like that. As soon as we enter the room we start making love. Non-stop.

THE WHOLE NIGHT? Monica asks, visibly green with envy.

Until dawn, Lucia proclaims.

Awesome!

Weren't you thinking about Jean-Claude?

How did you feel?

Our friend Lucia explains: Like any woman who's been fucked non-stop feels.

And that is?

Totally dazed and blissed out!

Holy cow! yours truly exclaims, losing her usual air of superiority.

And that's not all, she goes, rubbing it in, we wake up at two in the afternoon, breakfast in bed and then a shower together. Ralph says: I want you again. And we start fucking in the shower.

Again! Monica says, oozing envy.

What is he, an animal? goes Ale.

German men very passionate, very strong, asserts Beate.

And it didn't catch fire? asks Nadia.

How many times did you come? asks Betty.

Twenty-three, goes Lucia.

Get out! Seriously? asks Betty again.

But *how* did you come? asks Ale.

What do you mean? goes Lucia O'Connor.

No, honestly, since we're on the subject I'll tell you guys, I've never actually come . . . I mean . . . from penetrayshun alone, that is, goes Ale.

Because you're repressed, says Monica,

Do you always come? Valeria asks her.

Moneek proclaims: I gotta say, I always do. Front, back, everywhere.

Armpits, nose, elbows, Ale continues, messing with her.

Well, I'll tell you something, I've never come with a man, Betty declares, liberated at last by the second shot of herb-fortified grappa, adding: I only come when I do it myself. But once I slept with a woman and I came pretty fast.

Well then you picked the wrong team, honey,

No, it's true, a lot of women never let go when they're with men, Nadia says sounding like a psychologist on a television talk show.

I could never see myself sleeping with a woman, I don't know, it seems like something would be missing, says Ale.

That's obvious, goes Nadia.

I like everything, I proclaim.

There was never any doubt about that, adds Monica.

You're not gonna start lecturing me because I enjoy my sexuality, are you?

What the fuck's that supposed to mean?

No, really, the thing is some men think that as soon as they touch you with it you should have epileptic convulsions, declares Nadia.

Ale goes: If you don't start to twist and shout like a maniac after three seconds they get paranoid.

Hey, I've got one for you, Monica says. Once I was with a guy who annoyed the crap out of me and I told him so. I go, listen honey, try to stay calm because I never rip my hair out when I'm about to come, and don't think the second you come near me with it I'll start acting like an animal being slaughtered.

You didn't say that to the poor man, says Nadia.

Did he run?

He flipped out.

You're out of your mind,

No, really, there are some guys who don't get it at all, like I slept with this guy once, one of my professors actually (Ale is speaking) who was nice and all when he was vertical, but as soon as the horizontal time came, wham, he started saying come on, tell me you like it, tell me you like it, just like that, you know, without even a shred of preliminary activity.

Oh, no way, I'm all about passionate sex, there has to be passion, otherwise I tense up, Nadia says, I'm not saying you should only give it to your one true love, forget that, but, at least *during* there has to be pleasure, you know?

You know Sandrine, the cellist? Well, she told me she always comes, it hardly takes anything and she can even come ten times in one fuck.

If you ask me, she's frigid.

I say she's never come.

21.

Okay, but tell us more about the trip, Luci.

So far, you've only told us about the sex.

You felt pretty good, huh, riding around with the biker? asks Betty.

Lucia says: Other than the fact that my legs had turned to rubber and my back was a wreck . . . no, really, it's just that a kind of euphoria had come over me, we were driving through the Camargue, it was really beautiful, the white horses, the pink flamingos. We stopped to eat at a restaurant near a pond with flamingos, stuffed ourselves with fish, wine, sorbet. Even champagne. Oh, it was so nice! He held my hand the whole time, kissed me. When we got back on the motorcycle we were both pretty tipsy, we ended up on this really long beach at the mouth of the Rhone, it was practically deserted. The wind had changed, a pretty chilly mistral was blowing, then Ralph decided he wanted to go for a swim. I say, what? After all we ate! Him, ah-ha! We said no more fear, right? Me: okay, to hell with my paranoias, otherwise, what was the point of running off. We get undressed, I take a running start and dive into the sea.

Beate says: You Italians always afraid to swim after lunch, Italian mother ruins you.

Okay, cut it out, Beate.

The water's really cold, I'm not feeling so hot, my stomach's cramping, I'm short of breath, then I don't remember much, my head was spinning, maybe I fainted, I went under.

Oh my god, you almost kicked the bucket!

I don't know how long I was under, I swallowed a lot of water, Ralph saved me. I came to on the shore, I had chills and was shaking like a leaf. What a mess, man, he kept massaging me, he pulled a sweater over me, I was staring at my hands because they were yellowish-white. Then he pulled out a flask of whisky and made me take a big swig. After which, the niagara effect. I puked my guts out.

Unbelievable, Monica says.

I felt awful but I knew I was gonna make it. He's being really nice, holding me tight and saying he got really scared. Me too, I go, and him, I don't want to stay here any longer, let's go somewhere else. Feeling like the return of the living dead, I say: where the hell to? Him: let's go to Berlin.

Berlin? You went from the Camargue to Berlin? Nadia asks.

Wait, says Lucia, before we get to Berlin you have to hear about the other crazy stuff we did. We got lost three thousand times, we didn't even have a map, we went up to Lyon, we got lost again, I don't know where we ended up, in Clermond-Ferrand I think, Dijon, I don't know,

Were you feeling any better? asks Betty, concerned.

Not much. To make a long story short, the motorcycle broke down twice, we ended up on Lake Constance, and three days later in Vienna.

Why, were they giving away gas or something? says Nadia.

Pass me the mineral water, will ya, goes Monica.

Man, what a story, says Ale.

And that poor sociologist? You never called him? Never talked to him again?

Is that any way to behave?

Lucia continues: my back's killing me, my legs are all grimy, dust everywhere. In Vienna I say: are we stopping here or do we keep going until we drop? We found a room in a rather sinister-looking hotel, a soot-blackened little old building. I say: I'm just going to rest for a moment, okay. And I pass out. When I wake up it's dark outside, I look for him and he's not there. I don't know why, but I got all paranoid, I started thinking: he dumped me. He got sick of me, I'm a drag, hardly the kind of woman you'd run off on a motorcycle with. I was saying to myself, now what do I do? What the fuck am I doing here in a hotel in Vienna, without a dime in my pocket, without even knowing a word of German? I turn on the radio and jump in the shower, I remember a Tina Turner song was playing, and I started singing at the top of my lungs,

That's crazy, goes Nadia, I would have never expected it from you.

What?

It's crazy, she runs away from home, almost kicks the bucket, hooks up with some scumbag who dumps her in a hotel in Vienna, and what does she do: she starts singing at the top of her lungs!

Well, what should she have done?

Hey, have you guys seen the movie about Tina Turner's life?

Man, what a rough time that woman had,

All those beatings from Ike.

Thirty years of beatings and then she became a Buddhist,

Yeah, but she was still one gutsy lady, Tina was.

Do you guys think she was a masochist or was she really like that? Like what?

In love with the brute, obviously.

Go figure. Maybe she was in love some and liked to get beat some.

Well, listen to this, goes Lucia. When I get out of the shower, I find Ralph in the room,

Oh, so he didn't leave you, says Beate.

He listened to my entire singing performance, he's there laughing like crazy and he goes: I swear I've never heard anyone more off-key. I go: where have you been, Ralph? He comes up to me, takes off my towel and starts kissing me.

Ooh, enough already! Doesn't this biker know how to do anything else? says Nadia.

Hey, I wouldn't kick him out of bed, says Ale.

I say again: where have you been? Him: nowhere, I just went to see some people I know. I push him away and say: Ralph, I don't like the way we're living, like a couple of fucked-up losers.

Right, goes Betty.

What's the point of all this eating, drinking, me almost dying, wandering around like two lost souls, you trafficking in god knows what. What are you, a terrorist? Where did you get all that money? And how come you have dollars? I'm not some kind of cover for you, am I?

Cover for what? asks Nadia.

Lucia doesn't answer but keeps talking like Ralph's right in front of her: What are you, a drug dealer? A KGB agent?

The KGB doesn't exist anymore, goes Monica.

Plus, I'm here thinking you're gonna dump me any minute (still Lucia). Then, after I've been bitching at him for like ten minutes, all of a sudden Ralph pulls away like something bit him. He has a mean look on his face and says: you don't trust me at all. Me: well, no, you don't act like someone I can trust.

Yeah, right, you run off with a centaur and now you want to trust him too, says Monica.

Then Ralph says to me: and who can you trust, your boyfriend? And me, yes, I trusted Jean-Claude a lot, if you really want to know. Him: oh, so how come you're now a few thousand miles away from this know-it-all you trust so much?

He's right, why? repeats Betty, now hopelessly drunk.

Lucia: At this point I lose it, I start yelling and throwing my hands up in the air: oh what a fucking mistake! What a fucking mistake I made to leave Jean-Claude for you! I'm such an imbecile! I leave my boyfriend, my home, our beautiful memories . . .

If I had been Ralph, I would have kicked your ass, says Nadia.

Poor guy, hic, he must have felt so bad, hic, says Betty, who's gotten the hiccups.

Not that bad, says Lucia, he actually chewed my ass out big time. He lit a cigarette, exhaled, and then very calmly began to speak: listen to me, shithead. You've got Ralph right here in front of you, understand? Ralph, not some professor crazy about torture methods. Me: Jean-Claude isn't crazy about torture methods. He continues, totally serious: if you were so happy in your fucking bourgeois existence with all the shit you had in your head . . .

What shit? asks Beate.

Hic . . . goes Betty.

Listen, try taking nine sips of water while holding your nose, advises Monica, annoyed.

If you were so happy (Lucia continues, imitating her lover Ralph) with that know-it-all you trust so much and that other one who fucked guys right under your nose, what the fuck are you doing here, in an Austrian hotel, with some good-for-nothing asshole? You can go back whenever you want, I'm not holding anybody here, I've never kidnapped anyone, understand?

Dang! he really chewed your ass out, that biker guy chewed you out.

And then?

Nothing, I started to cry. I felt . . . you know: I'm a loser, what am I doing in this world, I'm stupid, no one loves me because I'm such a piece of shit . . . that kind of thing. Then I wanted to call Jean-Claude.

So why didn't you?

To be honest, I did, but nobody answered.

And then you left?

I sat there freaking out, he goes: I'm going out for a ride because all this has gotten me upset. Don't worry, I'm not going to disappear, blow your nose and put some of that crap on your face, tonight I'm taking you out on the town.

Hey, what a cool guy, hic, goes Betty.

Yeah, I like him, I really like him, goes Nadia.

Ale has switched to mineral water, she pours herself some and asks: So, did you make up later?

Nadia says: Did you like Austria? I find it so depressing!

Especially Vienna, it makes you want to shoot yourself, adds Monica.

What kind of trafficking did he do? Heavy stuff, I bet, right? asks Ale the detective.

Who was thinking about Austria, goes Lucia. I was totally wrapped up in my own paranoias, my life and my problems, I felt like I was in a Bergman film. But after we talked he didn't seem like he was mad at me anymore. That night we went to Grinzig, in the hills, we stuffed our faces like pigs, oh man, when I think about it, knödel, weiner schnitzel, tons of baked potatoes.

I love knödel, says Betty.

22.

THE AFTERNOON WE arrived in Berlin was so beautiful, says Lucia. Sunshine, fresh air, a turquoise sky. We stopped to have a snack in a big pastry shop, in the city center, on the Kudamm. There was a bunch of old ladies stuffing themselves with pastries and cakes. We're scarfing down cream puffs and liters of weak coffee ourselves. We keep kissing, and he asks me: are you doing okay? Me: I'm doing great. He goes: are you happy I brought you to Berlin? Me: really happy. Him: do you want to go back to the professor? Me: no. So we go over to his friends' who live in a squatter neighborhood, in the East, Prenzlauerberg.

What? asks Nadia.

A neighborhood with a bunch of buildings occupied by squatters. Ralph's friends are all real nice, there's a girl who's a gas-station attendant, Heidi, with shoulders this wide, she was with this Chilean guy, and then there was a Kurdish guy who lived with them, Abidin, the leader of the Kurdish Maoists. There were all kinds of people going in and out of the building, Kurds, Turks, South Americans, Maoist-Leninists . . .

Maoist-Leninists, Betty repeats slowly, as if she's supposed to memorize it.

What the fuck were you doing with those people?

I can't picture you with gas-station attendants and Turkish Maoists . . .

Oh, I made friends with the three girls who lived across from us, two Basques and an Italian. The Basques were nurses, the

Italian did tattoos. One afternoon they invited me over and we
became friends. Their place was a complete mess, a big table
in the middle of the room covered with leftover pizza, cartons,
empty beer cans, on the wall some bullfighting posters, Marilyn,
Greta Garbo, stuff like that.

It would have been better if you'd stayed home, comments
Betty the conservative.

Their names were Olga 1, Olga 2, and Milly. Milly, the one
who did tattoos, was covered with them. She did one on me too,

Where? asks Nadia, alarmed.

Here, she goes, turning her back and showing us a small
scorpion perched on her left shoulder blade. Then she continues:
The afternoon they invited me over, we sat on this pretty filthy
carpet, they made green tea and Milly pulled out some kind of
pipe. She goes: do you smoke? Me: oh no. Her: too bad. Me:
in any case, I certainly wouldn't smoke a pipe. This isn't a pipe,
it's called a chillum and you smoke drugs in it, she goes. What
drugs?! I go. It's nothing, goes Olga 2, don't scare her, it's light
stuff. And they start puffing away on the pipe. Olga 2 goes: are
you Ralph's girlfriend? I nod. Have you guys known each other
long? asks Milly, tossing her hair back before taking another hit
on this big pipe. She had hair down to her ass, bright red from
henna, but beautiful. I say, we've been together for almost a
week. Oh, goes Olga 1, anyway you guys make a handsome couple. So then I add, to tell you the truth I sort of had a husband,
but I've just run away from home, with Ralph. You ran away
from home? asks Olga 2. Exactly, I go. GUAPA! shouts Olga 1.
GUAPISSIMA! Olga 2 concurs. That increased my stock two
thousand points in their eyes. Is your husband boring? asks Milly.
Oh no, he's very intelligent, he's a sociologist, he's written some
books on penal systems, for example . . . Whatever, goes Milly,
and hands me the chillum.

Noooo!!! Don't tell me you smoked! goes Ale.

What a crowd, huh, says Monica.

I swear, after two hits I'm starting to feel pretty out of it,
my head's spinning, I ask: don't you guys have boyfriends? The

three exchange a look and Milly goes: we know how to enjoy ourselves without men, and she winks at me. Sometimes with men, too, adds Olga 1, but it's not the norm. I try to make an expression like I know what's going on, and we continue to smoke in silence. Milly goes: being a wife means denying yourself to satisfy other people's needs. Olga 1 adds: my mother always told me, Olga, remember that in marriage women have a lot to lose, as usual.

Lucia pours herself a drink, lights a cigarette and continues: Man, those girls told me all kinds of stuff. By the way, they're the ones who cut my hair, Milly did.

The criminal! goes Betty,

The two Olgas would go to the hospital, and I'd go to Milly's. I started asking her questions about Ralph, I wanted to know what he did for money. She got irritated, one day she goes: leave Ralph alone. He's a good guy, let him do whatever he wants, think about yourself a little. I go, oh, I stopped thinking about that a lifetime ago, about myself, I mean. And Milly, you've gotten yourself into a pretty bad place, huh. Then she looks me over and says: Let's see if we can't do something about that. First of all, I think you should spiff up a little. She gives me a pair of her jeans, old, all worn and ripped, which I wouldn't have even worn to clean the apartment in Paris, then she goes: go on, take off that miss-goody-two-shoes blouse. Before taking it off I go, could you turn around? She gets ticked off again and goes, jesus, you think I've never seen a pair of tits before? Then she says, take off your bra for a second, let me see, hmmm, not bad, they're bigger than they look . . . then she comes closer and touches my hair as if she were touching something useless and repulsive and goes: I'd change it, you have a thin face, you'd look good with short hair, what do you say?

And you? Did you let her?

Me? Yeah, I've always let other people do whatever they want to me. No, really, something happened . . . I let her cut my hair really short, I slipped on those trashed jeans, a T-shirt she gave me, and then I look at myself in the mirror and feel like crying.

I believe it, goes Ale.

You guys don't get it, it wasn't desperation, I was moved.

Moved? repeats Betty.

I saw something incredible in that mirror, sure, I felt ridiculous, I looked disheveled, scruffy, messed up,

Need any other synonyms?

So, I felt like crying,

You were that horrendous?

You don't get it, goes Lucia, I know it's not easy . . . okay: that was the first time I wasn't made up like a good little girl, like a miss goody-two-shoes, like Milly said. She really hit the nail on the head. I was confused, messed up, inside and out, and it was the first time my outside appearance matched what I felt on the inside. I kept looking at myself in the mirror and it was like I'd seen myself that way before,

You've lost me, goes Monica,

Lucia explains again: I was like that before, when I was a kid, when I was thirteen fourteen years old, I was like that, kind of dirty and scruffy.

23.

Dirty? Betty asks.

But I talked a lot, you know, I didn't always keep my mouth shut like now, I mean, like before I ran away, all meek and mild, damn it. I had short hair, as a kid, guess who my idol was?

Let's hear this too,

Suzy Quatro, you guys remember her?

Oh lord, I had actually repressed all memories of her, goes Monica.

Oh yeah, yeah, Suzy was great, I go, fuck yeah! I remember her, I had one of her records, what the hell was it called, I practically listened to it day and night.

Well, you know, that's what I was like, I didn't study, I got lots of F's, I wore Indian silk shirts, rings necklaces and bracelets, I wore patchouli,

That stuff was really gross,

You were right to lose that,

And I didn't have glasses, I didn't have gastritis, I ate junk, potato chips and ice cream, anything but organic food. I ate junk and I felt great, no gastritis whatsoever, man.

And then?

I flipped out, I started thinking about my entire life, from when I was a kid, when I'd cut classes to hang out with my friend, my best friend, her name was Annamaria, she was fat as a cow, I was really skinny,

That's classic, goes Nadia.

121

Man, we were so wild, continues Lucia, now unstoppable in her exterior monologue. She says: We'd spend the whole day gawking at boys, we'd go walking along the main drag and do nothing but devour boys with our eyes. Then we'd smoke in secret, we'd put on tons of make-up, I had some platform shoes that were six inches high, man, I still remember them, they were terrible, the top part was made of denim, the wedge of wood, and in the wedge I had carved, I Love You, stuff like that,

I did those things too, man, unbelievably tacky stuff, goes Monica,

Well, this may seem strange to you guys, but in our own small way, in our own provincial, tacky, small way we were real rebels. We didn't take any shit from anyone, we knew what we wanted, what we were going to do when we grew up. Annamaria wanted to be an attorney and defend the poor, abused women, the handicapped. I didn't ever want to get married, or have kids. I wanted to be in a rock band, like Suzy Quatro, with three or four guys playing with me, but I was the star. I was gonna tour the world with my band.

And then?

By the way, whatever happened to Suzy Quatro?

I'm not exactly sure what happened next, I can't tell you the exact moment I changed, when they beat me down. I started to study, I stopped yelling, fighting with my parents, with my teachers, I stopped staring at boys like a maniac, it must have been . . . I don't know . . . it was as if I felt I had to hide those things, I had to change them, it was inappropriate. All my feelings, my crazy ideas, my dreams, there was no one to tell me, okay, it's a bunch of crap but you have the right to think them, you have the right to want this . . . It's hard to say when it started, all I can tell you is that two years later, I found myself sitting in the front row, with glasses, a little blue skirt, a pony tail, and lots of good grades on my report card. I stopped getting my period, I didn't have it again for three years, to think that I was the first in my class to get it, at eleven and a half, even my boobs had started to grow . . . then it all disappeared, as if something had sucked everything back inside,

Hey, this is heavy stuff, Luci, goes Monica.

And there's another thing, I figured it out talking to Milly, because as soon as she cut my hair, the first thing I said was, oh god, will Ralph still like me? What if he doesn't like me anymore? And then she really laid into it, she goes: Listen, you sound like the type who's always wondering if other people like her.

Damn, she pegged you, this Milly pegged you dead on, I go.

She said to me: try turning it around, try to think about whether you like yourself the way you are, the way you feel. Try asking yourself if you like him, you know? Not just if he likes you.

Man, this Milly is really cool!

Was she pretty?

Who, Milly? Not in the conventional sense. Skinny as a rail, big mouth, big teeth, huge eyes, a sort of square face, but she's one of those women who look really beautiful even if they aren't,

Did she really say that to you?

Lucia continues and not even baby jesus could stop her: You know what I thought? I thought that at some point in my life, whatever I was wasn't working, no one liked me, so my real personality must have gone into hiding, and something that had nothing to do with me took my place. This something, this sort of voice, was constantly saying: okay, Lucia, this is a good job, working with books, it's the right thing to do, and here is a cultured intelligent and elegant man, you'd do well to behave in a way that will make him appreciate you and want to keep you. Be careful not to bother him too much and don't bore him with strange requests, don't talk too much about yourself, you're not that interesting. And so on. Even that pig Philippe, here's a writer, you love books, it's so nice that someone who writes books invites you out to dinner, make sure you behave and don't make a nuisance of yourself.

Shit, you figured all this out just by going to Berlin? asks Monica.

I've half a mind to hop on over there myself, goes Nadia.

Did you know that Nadia also had an affair she kept from us? I say.

I want to hear all about it later, goes Lucia perfunctorily, and then continues, Look, I was there in Berlin with people that Jean-Claude wouldn't have liked at all, that a lot of people wouldn't have liked, and I'd done one of the worst things a woman can do, run off with her lover, I dumped my almost-husband without saying anything to him, and you know what I thought? That it was the best thing I'd ever done in my life since I was fourteen.

What do you mean, a good man like that . . .

And your job? Series editor at Arrêt, that's no small feat . . .

Fuck that shit, I don't want to see those people again, not even in a photograph, you know . . .

Hey, how much can getting laid . . .

No, listen, you guys still don't get it: Ralph was a wonderful thing, maybe the best thing that's ever happened to me in my whole life, but I don't know if I'll stay with him, I . . . I . . . I think I need to be on my own for a while . . .

Are you sure you did the right thing breaking it off with Jean-Claude?

That's right, Monica's philosophy is never say anything,

Deny everything, even the evidence.

You guys can think what you want, but right now I feel like I've found myself, I'm full of energy, I feel like taking on the world, and I'm not going back, not for anything. That's what I was like when I was a kid, I hated doing things half-assed, maybe you're doing the right thing holding on to Paul and running around having affairs, I'm not telling you otherwise, I don't want to impose my point of view on anyone,

Careful, you're starting to talk like the pre-flight Lucia again, goes Ale,

No, seriously, everyone needs to do what they feel is best for them. I don't want to lie, I don't want to wear a mask anymore, not even if jesus christ himself asked me to do it.

Well don't tell me it's all the poor sociologist's fault,

No, I don't mean it's Jean-Claude's fault, when I met him I was already like that, I was already the fake Lucia. And he liked me precisely because I was the fake Lucia. He spends his time studying prison inmates,

Of course, they remind him of himself . . . I go, trashing poor J.-C.

Maybe he was a rebel as a kid too, what do I know, to be honest, I feel a little sorry for him, says Nadia.

No, look, if you ask me, Jean-Claude was born that way, with short hair, tortoise-shell glasses and a Foucault book under his arm, Monica trashes him further.

Come on, you really want to quit your job?

Girls, I've discovered that everything I thought was true and right up until today IS NOT! And there's no going back, you know!

Hey, how about some ice cream? You still like ice cream or are you against that too?

As long as it's not organic, says our newly cured friend Lucia.

24.

Wow, what a story, goes Ale.

We're all getting into some deep shit here, goes Monica.

It's all because of Venus in Scorpio, I explain.

You're always coming up with this astrological bullshit, goes Nadia.

Hey, thanks a lot, I go. Anyway, it's true.

What's true?

About Venus in Scorpio.

And what is this Venus in Scorpio supposed to do, goes Beate.

Heh-heh, I go, let me tell you, this year Venus will be in Scorpio for four months, and it'll influence everyone's lives, especially women's. It'll bring out your most hidden needs, repressed desires, inner conflicts, banished impulses of the soul, bottled-up emotions, and the good part is that it'll also give us the tools and the will to carry out all the crazy things we have in mind.

Nah, it's all bullshit, goes Nadia.

Hey, you guys do what you want, I warned you, I say, sibylline as hell.

Betty goes: No, come on, tell us more.

Here you have her, the psychic Miss Cleo, goes Ale.

You're a psychic? asks Beate.

Not exactly, I say, modestly.

For example, Lucia is a Scorpio, clearly a repressed Scorpio, as we learned from her big-time sex stories. Well, it's the sign that doesn't like doing things half way, as she just told us. Right now and in the months ahead it's likely she'll act impulsively, crazy stuff linked to sex, love and rock 'n' roll.

Come on, enough bullshit, okay,

What about Pisces? What happens to Pisces? asks Betty.

Pisces will reveal secret passions, many secrets, kind of a mess, actually, I don't see you doing so well.

Betty turns bright pink, puts her hands over her mouth and runs to the john. Nadia goes after her.

Oh shit! we hear, she threw up everything,

What a shame! My nice Sicilian pasta, says Ale.

I'm worried about Betty, goes Monica.

Since when do you worry about anything?

No, really, I don't know what's gotten into her, she's more out of it than usual, doesn't she seem that way to you?

And you, too, telling her you see trouble ahead, some friend, man,

Hey, it's not my fault, this is stellar stuff,

Yeah, stellar bullshit.

What happens to Capricorns? asks Ale.

No, uh-uh, I'm not telling you guys another fucking thing, because it always ends up being all my fault,

Nadia comes back and goes: Hey, she's sick, I'm taking her home.

What's wrong with her?

I need to go too, says Beate. When is Gianni coming home?

Oh god, I thought she'd forgotten about that, goes Monica.

I don't forgot anything, snaps Beate, who's definitely been hitting the bottle and whose aggressiveness is now resurfacing stronger than ever.

Listen, this is my place, goes Ale, with her hands on her hips, we gave you food and drink, you've gotten a load of our life stories, now chill out, it's not nice to keep rehashing it like this. I can always kick you out, you know.

Beate gets to her feet acting like someone who's spoiling for a fight. Meanwhile, Betty's back and she's about to launch herself into a rendition of an authentic hysterical fit.

Nadia goes to me: See, all because of you and those fucking zodiac signs.

Monica goes: Do something, for chrissakes. Then she grabs Betty by the shirt and slaps her a couple of times with those super-sized ex-basketball-player hands.

Betty stops screaming and starts to cry, buckets, as they say. Not even Nadia and Monica together can stop her, not even the virgin mary could stop her, from the looks of it.

Listen, forget what I told you about that Venus in Scorpio business, okay, I go. it's not like I'm an expert, come on, don't believe everything people tell you . . .

Betty continues to cry desperately and between tears she yells: I DON'T GIVE A FUCK ABOUT ASTROLOGYYYYY . . .

Okay, okay, so much the better, I say.

So what's gotten into you? asks Monica.

You haven't caught some strange tropical illness, have you? You never know . . .

Betty now looks more like Lucy from Charlie Brown than a flight attendant, her mouth is wide open and she's screaming: TROPICAL ILLNESS MY AA-ASS . . .

Jesus, she should be locked up, goes Lucia.

I'M PREGNANT! our flight attendant declares.

Holy hell, I go.

Holy shit, goes Monica.

Hey, come on, it's not a tragedy, look, there are a thousand solu—I'M PREGNANT WITH GIANNI'S BABYYYYY . . .

Ale and Beate, in unison: GIANNI WHO??!!

And Betty: Gianni Gianni. Gianni.

No, goes Ale, collapsing into a chair.

I don't believe it, goes Beate, standing up again with her hands reaching for our friend Betty's neck, and she really looks scary.

Monica goes to Betty's rescue, she tries to separate them, she says: Hey, what's this got to do with you, if anything it's Ale who should wring her neck.

But Ale is slumped in the chair, the color drained from her face, staring at the dinner leftovers like a madwoman.

It can't be, goes Nadia.

Why didn't you tell me, Betty? You could have at least told me, I go.

Yeah, the perfect person for keeping secrets, goes Monica.

Lucia goes: Wait a minute . . . s-so . . . how many months along are you?

Three, almost f-foouuuurrrr, actually, goes Betty, still crying.

Holy shit, I go.

Holy hell, goes Monica.

Are you sure? goes Lucia.

Didn't you go to that idiot, that doctor, says Nadia.

What doctor? asks Monica.

Yeah, when you skipped your period for two months, the guy who told you that loneliness in bed . . . what the hell was it he told you again?

Loneliness in bed is a form of alcoholism, the wretch repeats between sobs.

So?

Then when he figured out I was pregnant he said: I take back what I said.

Ah, you didn't tell me that part, you stopped mid-story, huh, says Nadia who evidently knows something we don't.

Yes, goes Betty, still sobbing.

Ale, say something, don't just sit there staring like that, goes Lucia.

Express your anger, Nadia advises her, like someone imitating her own analyst during a session at three hundred and fifty francs a pop.

Yeah, express it, goes Valeria.

Easy on the advice, girls, I suggest.

Fuck, how could you, says Ale, we've been friends a lifetime, with all the men around, you had to get yourself pregnant with mine, fuck, goddammit.

How could she, repeats Beate, with my man,

Hey, you take it easy, okay, goes Monica.

Well, this Gianni is remarkable, I go. Meaning a remarkable asshole.

Oh shut up, you, this is all because of your astrological obsession, Nadia insists.

How could you not have noticed anything, says Monica,

Well, you know what I think? goes Nadia, turning to Ale, if someone pretends to bury their head in the sand, they deserve what they get.

You're drunk, goes Lucia,

Ale begins to cry too, then she stops crying and starts grabbing the plates, forks and knives on the table and throws them as we all try to duck. Hey, are you out of your mind, goes Beate, trying to restrain her, but now Ale seizes the giant pasta bowl with the leftover eggplant, pepper, caper and anchovy sauce and throws it against the wall, she takes the cheese grater and flings it out the open window. From below we hear Maghrebian voices hurling insults in the original language.

Omigod, now they're gonna come up and murder us, goes Valeria.

Couldn't you two have minded your own fucking business, I go, express your anger, go ahead, express it . . .

Look, surely she noticed something, her guy and Betty have been having an affair since May, goes Nadia.

Since May! screams Ale,

What I'd like to know is who's the bitch here, I go.

How could you keep coming to Ale's dinners knowing what you knew, Monica asks Nadia.

Now look, the way I see it, if someone's stupid enough not to know her man has another woman then she deserves what she gets.

You're a real bitch, goes Monica.

What kind of friend are you? Beate says to Nadia.

By now I'm biting my tongue to keep from blabbing, I swear I'm dying to tell her everything, but I know I have to restrain myself, even though I'm not at all sober, even though none of us is, I tell myself I have to keep my cool.

Ale is going completely berserk, she's demolishing half the apartment. Now she's attacking the strings of garlic and hot peppers from Puglia, she's even pulled the famous good ceramic plates from the credenza and is hurling everything against the wall and out the window. What a scene, people!

When she's finished demolishing the demolishable, she turns to Nadia: As for you, you fucking bitch, didn't you ever realize that dead fish Hervé has been fucking her friend, the cellist, for the past year?

I yell: How the fuck did you know that? Who told you? (Then I think: Teresa! It has to be her, when she called, she talked to her first. Damn.)

WHAT!!?? goes Nadia, her eyes popping out of their sockets. You're lying, you just want to drag me down into the mud with you.

You're disgusting, girls, says Monica. You're acting like morons,

No, now you're going to tell me everything you know, goes Nadia.

I only know what Teresa told me, that your boyfriend went to Sandrine's.

That bastard! says Nadia. And he even made me feel guilty. That son of a bitch! And I was the one who didn't feel like fucking, right! I'll kill him.

Holy fuck, goes Lucia.

Just wait and see, I'm gonna kick his ass! says Nadia rushing to the door. She grabs her coat then comes up to me: The slut's address.

Wait, what's she got to do with it? goes Monica.

You don't go around screwing other women's men, goes Nadia.

Look who's talking, I go.

I'm coming too, shouts Beate,

What's this got to do with you?

Can I come too? asks Betty.

You better cool it, honey, goes Monica.

25.

WE GO OUT into the street, it's almost two-thirty. We head toward boulevard Rochechouart and after crossing Pigalle, we go down rue des Martyrs, where Sandrine lives.

I ring the bell and after a good while Teresa answers the buzzer. Who is it? she asks. Teresa, can you open the door? It's me, I'm with my friends. What I hear on the intercom is: Oh holymotherofgod. We enter the courtyard and a light goes on inside Sandrine's place. Teresa is wearing a nightgown that's all lace and ruffles, and with her dark curls she looks like an imitation of Scarlett O'Hara.

Where'd you find the nightgown? I've never seen you in a getup like that.

Oh, Sandrine lent it to me. She's got a collection of vintage nightgowns that look right out of a Barbara Cartland romance, I swear.

Hey, does this seem like the time to chat about nightwear? goes Monica.

Where's the slut? asks Nadia.

I've already heard that line, goes Betty.

Do me a favor, shut up, Ale says to her. Try to let me forget you even exist,

What the hell's going on here? asks Teresa.

That was really smart, telling Ale everything, I go.

HUH? goes Teresa O'Hara, still out of it.

Wasn't it you who told Ale about Sandrine's affair with Hervé?

Yeah, well she's a real bitch if she went and told her! she says in her own defense.

Way to go, my compliments, goes Monica.

What the fu— what are all you guys doing here? You've been drinking, haven't you?

Listen, hand over the cellist, because I'm gonna shove her cello you know where.

Hand her over, repeats Beate.

What the hell have you got to do with this,

Jesus, don't make me crazy. Sandrine's not here, this is the apartment, you can see for yourself, right?

OH! IT'S THREE A.M. AND THEY STILL HAVEN'T COME BACK!!! goes Nadia.

Okay, listen girlfriend, today was a really shitty day, I wouldn't mind getting a couple hours sleep, goes Teresa.

What happened to you? goes Lucia.

Geez, Lucia, what the fuck did you do to your hair? I hardly even recognized you! What the hell did you do?

She ran away, goes Betty, with a German biker, and she left her boyfriend.

WHAT? says Teresa, wait, somebody pinch me, maybe I'm still dreaming, and look at you, Betty, jesus you've gotten fat, she makes a point of noticing.

Teresa, forget about Betty, please, I say.

Seriously, you guys are all freaking out, what is it, the Paris air doesn't agree with you? Anyway, if anyone should be freaking out here it's me.

What happened to you? Lucia asks again.

Oh, nothing, a minor issue, I was supposed to marry this Algerian guy and this afternoon I got a call from some girl who's pregnant with his baby, that's all, an insignificant little detail . . .

Oh crap, goes Monica.

More pregnancies? You Italian women don't know use of cotraceptives? asks the German.

Contraceptives, I go.

No, it's because we have the pope, you know, the church . . . goes Ale.

You're out of your mind, goes Nadia.

Hey, listen, the chick was this really thin, blonde French girl with a cute turned-up nose and all, Teresa clarifies, these clichés about Italy have nothing to do with it, okay?

Please, says Monica.

Cheating is an international reality.

Why are we standing here? Let's sit down at least,

You got anything to drink? asks Ale.

When is the cellist coming back? asks Nadia.

Why, what are you going to do to her?

Listen, you can't be too pissed at Hervé now. What about the story with the bioenergist? How do we explain that?

What a dumbass I was! I told him everything. I must have gone through, like, three thousand guilt trips. That bastard enjoyed the hell out of my guilt, and meanwhile he was fucking the cellist, can you believe that?

Yeah, well, think about Ale then. It's even worse for her. She believes in fidelity, what about her,

Hey, let's not go there, goes Monica, lighting a cigarette, and adds: Oh, by the way, that reminds me of a joke, you guys wanna hear it? Here goes. So, there's this guy who's feeling really tired, really down, and he goes to the doctor. The doctor examines him and notices that the guy's dick is all messed up, completely trashed, and he goes: hey, you must have an incredible sex life! Are you married? How many times a week do you make love with your wife?

What happened to Alessandra? asks Teresa, interrupting Monica's joke.

No, really, let's not go there,

Ale starts crying again. Monica goes: Oh no . . .

When is Sandrine coming back?

Did you really run away from home? Teresa asks Lucia again.

Girls, if I had it to do all over again I'd sew it up, or become a nun.

Stop talking crap.

Come on, you guys wanna hear this joke, or what? So then the doctor goes: how many times a week with your wife? With my wife? he goes. Nothing unusual, no more than two or three times a week. And the doctor, strange, that doesn't make any sense. Listen, do you by any chance have . . . a lady friend? A lady friend? Yes, he goes. Ah, so you overdo it a little with her then. How many times a week do you make love with your lady friend? Uh, look, the normal, no more than two-three times a week . . . Okay, I haven't made myself clear, then . . .

Hey, Teresa, dig up something to drink, there must be something to drink in this place.

Teresa starts rummaging around in the fridge and pulls out a bottle of beaujolais nouveau. There's this, she says, and adds: We need to come up with a way of doing without men.

No, the point isn't doing without men, it's knowing how to make asses of them like they do to us.

What clichés!

Beaujolais nouveau is awful, I go. Tomorrow we'll all be hungover,

Look, I think we will be regardless,

Tomorrow . . . tomorrow is already here,

Come on, open that bottle.

You guys think we'll all end up alcoholics?

Come on, how does the joke end,

The joke: the guy goes: listen, maybe it's because I also have this friend . . . and, you know, sometimes the two of us get together, sometimes his wife too, all three of us . . . Ah! goes the doctor, and does this happen often? No, no more than two three times a week.

I don't see where the fun would be without men.

That's for damn sure.

No, really, the point is we need to change, we need to learn to be free, not to allow anyone to close off our horizons.

Yeah, some horizons.

I say: if we learned to face the fact that there is no arm to cling to, but that we go alone and our relation is to the world of reality (when I'm drunk quotes from old Virginia Woolf come to me quite easily).

You guys want some chamomile tea by any chance?

Chamomile! Nobody's got an upset stomach.

Anyway, let me tell you guys the end of the joke. So, no more than three times a week with the wife, no more than three times a week with the mistress, ditto with the friend and the friend's wife. So the doctor looks at him with concern and says, my dear fellow, don't you realize that you're destroying yourself with your own two hands? And the man goes: With my hands? No, no more than two three times a week . . .

Nadia, who was drinking, suddenly bursts out laughing, spraying wine all over Monica's skirt.

Hey, careful with my skirt, I just got it!

Man, what a story, goes Ale,

Hee hee, no more than two three times a week, repeats Beate.

Who was this guy? asks Betty.

Hey, does this seem like a good time to pull out a joke like that?

Come on, you need to know how to downplay things in life. Pass me some of that crummy beaujolais, will ya,

Downplay? I feel like killing someone.

So what happened to Betty anyway? asks Teresa.

She's pregnant.

You too! No! Listen, if Samir got you pregnant too, don't tell me, okay, I don't want to know, I've had enough for today,

Oh no, don't worry, you're not good enough friends for her to screw your man, says Ale.

What is that supposed to mean? says Teresa.

Now the atmosphere is a bit more relaxed, as in the calm after the storm. Ale and Valeria are sitting on the floor leaning against the wall. Monica is sitting on the floor too, with the bottle of beaujolais between her legs. Betty is seated on a chair, drying her face.

Valeria says to Lucia: I didn't understand whether you ever talked to the sociologist again.

And the biker? Whatever happened to that hunk?

Ralph stayed in Berlin.

Are you going to see him again? Do you guys still talk? You're not going to let him slip away are you, that big hunk of beef, I mean, two hundred pounds of love.

No, you got it wrong, that was the bioenergist,

What?

It was the bioenergist who weighed two hundred pounds,

I want to change everything, Lucia says again, maybe I'll leave Paris.

Where the hell will you go?

I don't know yet.

Listen, I don't get what this whole fucking thing did for you, asks Monica.

Yeah, maybe now you'll find yourself without a man and without a lover, says Nadia.

Well, at least she'll have some peace and quiet, goes Valeria.

Hee, too funny, no more than two three times a week, goes Betty, who's still a couple of lines behind.

One of these days I'm gonna kill her, goes Nadia.

Oh, you! goes Ale.

Yeah, but if you leave Paris, you won't have your friends to listen to all your stories, says Monica.

Maybe that would be a relief, I say.

Moron, goes Ale.

So, you haven't decided anything yet?

No, or maybe I have.

Don't you have another joke that'll make us laugh like the last one? goes Betty.

I don't understand all that stuff about running away, Monica says again, really, guys, I don't get it.

Whatever, says Ale, draining the dregs in her glass, so how do you feel now?

Well, I've changed, haven't I? goes Lucia.

Misfits, Oddballs and Outcasts: The Fabulous Women of Rossana Campo
Adria Frizzi

Often referred to as one of the "bad girls" of contemporary Italian literature earlier in her career, Rossana Campo (1963-) enjoys unique popularity in Italy thanks to a very personal style that relies heavily on the colloquial, spoken register and her focus on the female voice and experience. Her production ranges from novels, short stories and journalism, to children's literature, theatre, and painting. Her debut novel, *In principio erano le mutande* [In the Beginning Was Underwear], published in 1992, was made into a film of the same title, directed by Anna Negri in 1999. Fifteen novels and short story collections, three books for children, a radio drama, and one Young Adult novel followed, establishing Campo as one of the most original authors in contemporary Italian literature. Her novel *Dove troverete un altro padre come il mio* [Where Are You Going to Find Another Father like Mine], a foray into the territory of autofiction, was awarded the prestigious Premio Strega Giovani and the Elsa Morante Prize in 2016. The publication list of this prolific author continues to grow, with a novel, *Così allegre senza nessun motivo* [So Happy Without a Reason] and a book on autobiographical writing. *Scrivere è amare di nuovo* [To Write Is to Love Again], published in 2019.

Campo's literary formation has been linked to her work under the neo-avant-garde poet Edoardo Sanguineti in her college days,

and the Giovani Cannibali [Young Cannibals], a group of dis-
parate young writers who came to the fore in the early 1990s,
with whom she shared a search for a new approach to the novel
through linguistic experimentation and transgressive themes.

After reaching a wide audience with her first book, Campo
quickly became a controversial literary figure, praised and exco-
riated alike for her uncensored stylistic choices and themes. The
main focus of Campo's early novels has been defined as "what
women discuss when men are not around." Her humorous and
ironic depictions of identity, sexual and emotional issues typical
of the female experience, her quirky characters, and her uniquely
vibrant, quotidian and incisive language account for her success
in the literary marketplace as well as the interest she has gener-
ated among scholars and critics.

While Campo's more recent work often displays darker tones,
she has remained true to her original stylistic and thematic
choices, deepening her examination of the female experience
and voice through occasional excursions into different subgenres,
such as children's and young adult's books, detective/noir fiction,
and the memoir.

Never Felt So Good (1995) is Campo's third novel, after *In
principio erano le mutande* and *Il pieno di super* [Fill 'Er up with
Premium, 1993]. These books are viewed by some as a trilogy of
sorts in which Campo fleshes out her literary project. All three
narratives are centered on female sexuality and revolve around
the conversations of a group of girlfriends at different stages of
their lives.

Linguistically, the writing is characterized by the reliance on
a heavily spoken, "low" register filled with colloquialisms and
slang, and an unconventional use of spelling and punctuation
that highlights the immediate and irrepressible quality of the
women's ongoing conversation stream. Campo's campy blend of
pop culture and colloquial style includes music, literary and film
references that are equally marked by the rejection of stuffiness,
conventional canons and expectations.

Part and parcel of her approach to literature is genuine

accessibility, which includes an active and ongoing relationship with readers through her publisher's blog first, and her Facebook page later. This pursuit of accessibility on both the literary and the personal front accounts for the iconic status Campo enjoys in Italy and throughout Europe, as her books' impressive print runs (*Mai sentita così bene* is now in its fifteenth edition, with a total run of 100,000 copies) and translations into several languages, including French, Spanish, Dutch, German, Portuguese, Greek and Romanian, indicate.

In spite of Campo's popularity in Europe, her work remains largely unknown in the U.S. My personal observations confirm the apparent disconnect between Europe and the U.S., and seemingly between readers and publishers within this country, at least on the empirical level. While Campo's writing has consistently captivated scholars as well as students, colleagues and other readers, the American literary establishment's (publishers and literary agents alike) perceptions of Campo's writing appear to be largely based on the fact that it doesn't fit familiar but rigid and often obsolete categories and expectations (literary vs. commercial; canonical vs. experimental; highbrow vs. lowbrow) or even established genres and subgenres (fiction vs. theatre or film script; romance, confessional, chick lit, etc.). This disconnect points to the politics of publishing, diffusion, text reception, and censorship. While the silencing of female voices may no longer be as intractable a problem as it was in the not so distant past, issues of dominance and power in the shaping of a literary canon remain critical in any discussion of the diffusion of individual authors and literatures that challenge old and new hierarchies alike.

Indeed, Campo's literary project hinges upon a new non-hierarchical vision that eschews acritical deference towards tradition and strongly focuses on orality:

> What I'm trying to do with my writing is to deliver maximum force and energy. In order to do this I've always tried to eliminate everything that sounds fake, cloying,

sappy, literary and stuffy to me. It's because of this pre-occupation that a large part of my work consists of the attempt to transfer the power of the spoken language onto the written page. If a page is "well-written" but sounds literary and lifeless, it has no interest for me.[1]

Implicit in this search is a keen political awareness of the trajectory of Italian literature and the rejection of anything that is perceived as lifeless and an instrument of oppression:

> I have to say that the history of Italian literature, as far as prose, and especially the novel, go, is very lacking from the linguistic point of view. Aside from a few felicitous instances—Boccaccio, Dante, who were trying to renew the language—there are many centuries where the literary language is an artificial language. The language of the ruling classes, full of Latinisms—a language for priests.[2]

In this context, orality is understood in the broadest sense, as an approach to writing that is comprised of both stylistic and thematic features:

> What matters to me is that the stories I tell have energy and power. I believe that this is attainable by working on orality, on the spoken language. I'm interested in a language (and therefore a story) that is carnal, corporeal, physical, humoral. I'm interested in madness, sex, despair, and vitality.[3]

Never Felt So Good unfolds during a dinner party among girlfriends, all of whom are, like Campo herself, Italian expats

---

[1] Quoted by Stefania Lucamante, 'Una laudevole fine: femminismo e identificazione delle donne nella narrativa di Rossana Campo.' *Italianistica* 2/3 (2002), 296.

[2] Quoted by Johanna ten Cate, *La scrittura particolare di Rossana Campo: tradurre il linguaggio parlato*, MA Thesis, 2008, p.11.

[3] Johanna ten Cate, p. 12.

living in Paris. They are celebrating the return of Lucia after she has ditched her respectable lover, prestigious career, and straight-laced life to run off with a German biker. During the course of the evening, all recount their amorous adventures and affairs among laughter, tears, and a few big surprises. The novel ironically inscribes itself in the fabulating tradition of *The Thousand and One Nights*, Chaucer, and Boccaccio by allowing each of the women to take center stage and spin her tale in an irrepressible and often raucous wordfest. Indeed, while the characters are captivating and their stories funny and enthralling, ultimately "the real actors are the words, and what dominates the stage is language."[4]

The result is a polyphonic text driven by dialogue that blurs genre distinctions between novel, theater and film script[5] and is marked by the transgression of classic narrative and structural patterns and linguistic codes. This includes eschewing conventional rules of punctuation and spelling such as use of quotation marks, capitalization, and the deformation of words alike to reflect the way they are (mis)pronounced, all features that have become trademarks of Campo's style. In particular, the use of a simple comma, or even no punctuation at all, in lieu of the traditional quotation marks to signal a change in speaker creates a cascading effect of criss-crossing and overlapping voices, themes and thoughts that privileges and celebrates orality in all its untamed glory.

The anti-hierarchical, subversive approach to structure, theme, and style, is also seen in the countless references to books, music, film, and cultural trends, ranging from Tolstoy and Woolf to the Addams family. In this sense the novel is also a cultural palimpsest, marked by an irreverent and omnivorous approach through which Campo's women appropriate and recontextualize high and pop culture alike in order to understand their experiences and reclaim their voice and visibility.

My overall guiding principle as a translator in approaching

---

[4] Angelo Guglielmi, back cover blurb, *Mai sentita così bene*, Milano: Feltrinelli, 1995.

[5] See Marina Romero Naranjo, "Una novela para leer en voz alta," *Espéculo*, 2002.

Campo's writing has been to avoid normalizing, explaining or cleaning it up. The difficulties of translating this author boil down primarily to finding ways of rendering in English her rich mix of linguistic and expressive registers and, occasionally, other languages. While hitting the right tone is undoubtedly challenging, the writing itself, as often is the case, also provides the translator with a clear roadmap. Thus, many of Campo's stylistic quirks, such as the lack of capitalization or punctuation, or the use of capitals to convey emphasis or shouting, remain largely unchanged. The phonetic spelling of some words required minimal adjustments in the switch from the Italian to the English sound system: for example, the French name Monique, transcribed in Italian as Monik, became Moneek in English. The pronunciation of the English word "penetration," rendered in Italian as "penetrascion," became "penetrayshun" in English, and so on. Beate's German accent and occasional ungrammatical utterances were similarly easy to recreate. I also hewed fairly closely to Campo's mix of slang, profanity and ironic use of an elevated register and the deliberate way in which she uses iterations of the verb to say (go, comment, conclude, observe, inquire, declare, state, exclaim, etc.) as a clipped form of stage directions.

Not surprisingly, the greatest challenges are found in the area where culture and language intersect, especially in the case of slang and idiomatic expressions. The use of religiously flavored interjections is much more common in Italian, and the number of variations much higher, so at times it was necessary to walk a fine line between maintaining a critical feature in the voice of characters like Ale, and finding a plausible English equivalent.

Along the same lines, some allusions had to be adjusted to the English-speaking reader's cultural reference range—thus, for example, the ironic mention of Amedeo Nazzari as an obsolete matinée idol was replaced with Errol Flynn, a fairly close equivalent both in terms of image, star-status and generation.

I'm eternally grateful to Rossana Campo for her fabulous women, for her unique writing, and for the inspiration and pleasure she has brought me, both as a reader and as a translator. My sincere thanks go to Traci Andrighetti for introducing me to this novel and for her collaboration in the early stages of the translation. I also wish to acknowledge all the students, friends, colleagues and the countless other people who read, discussed, and offered suggestions and support over the years. Special thanks, as always, to REYoung and the Savages for their invaluable editorial advice and for reading every single draft of this translation. Για σας.

Adria Frizzi
Austin, Texas, June 2019